LEDA

LEDA

A Novel

A.A. EIMONT

Abbott Press books may be ordered through booksellers or by contacting:

Abbott Press
1663 Liberty Drive
Bloomington, IN 47403
www.abbottpress.com
Phone: 1-866-697-5310

ISBN: 978-1-4582-1612-0 (e)
ISBN: 978-1-4582-1611-3 (sc)

Printed in the United States of America.

Abbott Press rev. date: 7/14/2014

LEDA AND THE SWAN

A SUDDEN BLOW, THE GREAT WINGS BEATING
STILL ABOVE THE STAGGERING GIRL, HER THIGHS
CARESSED BY THE DARK WEBS, HER NAPE CAUGHT
IN HIS BILL, HE HOLDS HER HELPLESS BREAST
UPON HIS BREAST

HOW CAN THOSE TERRIFIED VAGUE FINGERS PUSH

THE FEATHERED GLORY FROM HER LOOSENING
THIGHS? AND HOW CAN BODY, LAID IN THAT
WHITE RUSH,

BUT FEEL THE STRANGE HEART BEATING WHERE
IT LIES?

A SHUDDER IN THE LOINS ENGENDERS THERE

THE BROKEN WALL, THE BURNING ROOF AND
TOWER AND AGAMEMNON DEAD.

BEING SO CAUGHT UP,

SO MASTERED BY THE BRUTE BLOOD OF THE
AIR, DID SHE PUT ON HIS KNOWLEDGE WITH HIS
POWER

BEFORE THE INDIFFERENT BEAK COULD LET HER
DROP?

William Butler Yeats

Reprinted by permission of United Agents on behalf of Caitriona Yeats

CHAPTER 1

Leda enveloped in silence, dreamed of jagged red rocks against a purple sky. She floated in a caressing sea of sand, felt the warm wind on her face and smelled the parched, pure air that held the aroma of rosemary. Silence—a heavy, profound presence smothering all that was shallow, distracting, and inconsequential. Silence was not the absence of sound; it was the presence of the eternal.

As the sound of lawn mowers woke her, she murmured, "Damn". *Silence is unobtainable. I should start a class action suit against noise pollution; it is more harmful than second hand smoke - noise harms minds and souls.*

Leda, stretching in bed, glanced at a painting, a gift from Aliyah on their bedroom wall. The artist depicted a Bedouin life of desert, tents, camels and sheep. She imagined herself there, shrouded in a burka. *Aliyah knew I would love the painting. It would be another life, a totally different perspective on all my beliefs. We discussed the possibility of doing medical charity work together. Going to the Middle East would stop my useless reading, thinking and philosophizing. It would spurt me into action again. I've been at a loss since I stopped my medical practice. Thinking without action is useless.*

She wrapped herself in a green silk robe, and headed to the kitchen for coffee. After breakfast Leda enjoyed daily routine of grooming: the perfumed shower, the clean slick teeth, and the transformation of the canvas of a plain face with creams and colors into a pleasing portrait. She loved herself because in life she had been well loved. To avoid the indignities of a declining life, she tried her best to be attractive but it was not with the desire to be young. "If you have an historic, two hundred year old house and you make improvements and paint it and restore it, you are not pretending that it is new construction." *A woman with no care for upkeep is like an abandoned house, an eyesore. The most brutal aspect of aging is not even found in the physical changes, but the mental ones— the unattractive hesitancy, the fear, the lack of confidence that exemplifies the prime is past.*

Time—the beginning climb followed by a peak, and then the rapid descent. Was it the force of gravity that hastened the downward slide? Was there a relationship of time to gravity? Certainly gravity affects my wrinkles and bones. The subjective quantification of time—a week at age ten is not a week at age eighty and there were no landmarks at all for the coming decades, only a world shrinking in possibilities. I could live thirty more years becoming entirely invisible in a pinpoint of available options. Have all the important things already happened?

She was forever preparing, pruning her life for some future blooming so she was injured by the idea that it was all over. *How can my contemporaries define themselves in terms of being a retiree, or a grandparent or an illness? This was admission of defeat, a death before dying. In certain cultures we would be revered, having authority, giving advice, guidance. Now nothing is as useless as something old; everything is disposable, few objects deserved repair. Nothing is as useless and beyond repair as people over sixty-five and I am a victim of the prevailing ethos.*

"Arthur is coming home from Montana today." she said to Rhoda the housekeeper as she checked the flights.

"You sure did miss him. You have the best husband I ever did see." Rhoda answered as she slowly cleared the table.

Driving to the airport the absence of the Trade Towers was still a void in the skyline. The news blared how the survivor's families were fighting over the billions in compensation. *Yet soldiers dying for our country in the Middle East got ten thousand dollars.* An SUV flying a tattered American flag passed her. *A more patriotic action would be driving more energy efficient cars leading to different policies in the Middle East. Justice, does it exist at all? Do the political interests of the rich and powerful always trump the interests of the poor and helpless? Is there any moral superiority to being the underdog?*

Reaching the hub of modern travel, she parked and went inside as a woman in a lime green suit with a brown leathery face walked by. In the past women used parasols and wore hats and gloves to prevent sun damage. Before Muslim women took on the burka as a religious symbol of modesty, it had its origins in beauty. The lighter the skin the higher the value of any woman in a culture, and in the sun-scorched desert, the only way to preserve the beauty of a fair skin was complete coverage. And then this bow to beauty became a

3

symbol of oppression. Just as in the past breaking the foot bones of Chinese women for the beauty of tiny feet impeded walking.

Corsets and tight-bodiced dresses should come back into fashion. When eating with any type of girdle or stays digging into the body, an inordinate amount of food signals discomfort. No wonder that the huge sweatpants, elastic waistlines and huge tee shirts allowed everyone their "supersized" portions in ultimate comfort. I must be very sensitive to visual pollution.

"Arthur!" Leda started running toward him in the line of disembarking passengers.

"You didn't have to pick me up, I could have taken a cab," said Arthur, embracing her.

Observing him in western wear with new cowboy boots and a black cowboy hat rakishly shading his eyes she wanted to tell him he looked sexy but the swirling crowds of people were in the way and she led him towards the Exit sign. She turned and asked, "What were economic conditions in the West?"

Arthur was laughing as he followed her. "I had forgotten how serious you are."

She turned around and kissed him. They exited into acres of parked cars when Leda instantly noticed her Mercedes. Walking toward the car, Arthur took the keys from Leda. "How was Montana?" Leda asked as she expertly slid into the passenger seat.

"It is still America – pure, young, and vibrant. It is only in New York that the real facts of our civilization become apparent. I have real fears about our future." Arthur lit a cigarette and pulled out of the hourly parking lot.

"I just finished an interesting book. The life of empires has a curve—nations are young, have a peak, and then a decline. Sir John Glubb outlined this theory. His conclusion was that the decline of empires is always associated with the rise of women in power; they leave the home and child rearing and this destroys the nucleus of the family. Without strong families, the peak is passed and the decline starts."

Arthur smiled, "Yes, I remember that book, I read it long ago but it was not only women's role in society that was responsible. It was always the many wars at the borders of the empire and a devaluation of the currency to fund those wars."

They rode in silence for a while listening to John Adams' Nixon in China. After small talk about household concerns, with a giant bill from their gardener being the main topic, Leda was looking out the window at a deserted landscape of green lawns, picture perfect homes, and an occasional nanny pushing a toddler in a stroller, or a pained jogger.

"Arthur, what do you think of Islam?"

"Leda, stop talking about religion and politics!" Arthur said as he reached over and touched her cheek. "Let's talk about sports or sex!"

"You know the only things worth talking about are religion and politics. That way you discover a person's philosophy, their mind and soul. Sex and sports are not topics of conversation, but activities to be indulged in." Seeing his serious expression, she added, "Sex will be more than talk very soon," and Arthur started laughing as the car entered the enclave of Greenwich, Connecticut.

The driveway shaded by large oak trees, lined with a profusion of Rhododendrons led to a three story brick Tudor house. With luggage in hand they entered the interior of silver and crystal with Persian rugs, fresh flowers and the aroma of furniture polish. The massive living room walls held an enormous collection of books on eclectic topics. A small, blond cairn terrier ran up jumping on Arthur. "Have you been protecting Leda, Frodo?" exclaimed Arthur, lifting the dog to receive a doggy kiss. " A man in Montana told me that dog owners need love whereas cat owners want to give love. Is that why we have both?"

A black and white cat came and Leda picked him up. "Knowing Felix, I would say I agree. There are people who love animals to the extent that animals are their best friends, they understand, love, and appreciate them. However, these animal lovers do not like other humans as much or have sympathy for their pain. Hitler loved animals and was a vegetarian but was willing to kill millions of humans. There should be a term for that, homosapiensphobia- a hatred of mankind."

Rhoda met them with small sandwiches and iced tea. "It's great to see you back, Mr. Lodge. And that tan looks mighty good on you. You've lost some weight." They settled into the sofa in the large white and beige living room since Leda wanted the people to stand out and not compete with furniture and walls. She was dismayed at unattractive people in her house as if they were upsetting her composition of life.

"You really picked the most desolate state in the country. I know you always wanted to visit there because of your early years. Why go alone?"

Arthur, sipping his iced tea said, "At my age it is important to process life and it is best to do that alone. After all, everyone must come to terms with their own life."

"How was travel in a pick-up truck?" Leda said to avoid the unpleasant thought of Arthur's mortality.

"I thought that with my rented red pick-up and my western wear I could blend in. I stopped for breakfast where there was a whole line of pick-ups. As I went in I took off my hat but not before I noticed everyone else had a hat on. So I scratched my head and put it back on. When in Rome do as the Romans do. Then I went up to the buffet and took a bowl full of what looked like oatmeal. When the waitress thanked me for my tip she said she never did see anyone eat so much of their cream gravy."

"See that is what you get for pretending you are one of the 'good ole boys'."

Leda, laughing, took Arthur by the hand and led him upstairs. Leda took off her makeup and creamed her face as Arthur took a shower. "Your turn." Arthur said as he walked into the bedroom with a towel around his waist. "I was hoping you would join me."

A pensive Leda was looking at herself in the mirror, "I also want to examine my life and make it mean something. I want to achieve something significant." Leda said in all seriousness.

"You will achieve more if you get into that shower or I will carry you there!" said Arthur laughing as he chased her into the bathroom.

CHAPTER 2

At breakfast the next day, Arthur handed Leda the New York Times "Look at this headline: PEDOPHILE PRIEST FORGIVEN. I know you are a serious Catholic but this scandal must shake your faith."

Leda took the paper and read the article with a frown, "I think that the Church is made of fallible humans, but this does not detract from the basic teachings. It is a scandal and will be an excuse for all those who find the teachings too strict. As for myself, what choice do I have? When a starving person receives food do they ask for a list of the ingredients, the qualifications of the chef, or worry about allergies? No! They grab whatever they can get and gobble it down. What else but religion gives an explanation for this dastardly, unfair and even evil existence?" Leda dumped the paper into the trash and dressed for church.

Mass at St. Mary's had guitar music and a youth choir with a primitive sound from the Top 10. The priest, in Oprah imitation, walked the aisles and solicited comments from the parishioners to chuckles and laughter. His sermon began: "What a beautiful day the Lord has made. Turn to your neighbor and give them a big smile. Smile. Yes, that is what the Lord wants you to do. Can anyone give me a reason why they are smiling?" He pointed to a teenage boy with severe acne. "You, why are you smiling?"

The boy turned a bright red and mumbled, "Because you told us to." The congregation broke out in hilarious laughter. Leda cringed.

The sacred ritual of the bread and wine becoming the body and blood of Christ, performed by the priest facing the congregation, took on the aspects of a cooking show. Even the human aspects did not receive adequate thought because the priests never related to any authentic matter of moral concern. Although contraception and abortion were frequently alluded to in obscure terms such as "right to life," there was never any mention of the church's stand on tax evasion, or current morality, or artificial conception, or cloning, or the politics of war, or assisted suicide. *A miracle deserves a proper setting - shrouded in incense, with ancient sacred chants. Then the soul is uplifted and a true union can occur between the human and the divine. But not in this afternoon TV show.*

As she was leaving the church, a middle-aged lady in a grey dress with a little headscarf and a large crucifix was collecting money for the homeless. The man in front of her greeted her as Sister Alice. Leda remembered her ethereal looking nuns in their long black robes and white starched wimples. *What a tragedy to go from the high style of saintliness into the dumpiness of the commonplace. Perhaps all these are superficial to the spirit. But we still deal with the externals with our senses.*

The afternoon was a jumble of phone calls and a golf game for Arthur. Leda went to the gym where her favorite trainer put her muscles through an exceptionally difficult workout. Leda said that he was being cruel to an old lady but Dominick, a muscle-bound youth, just laughed, "You're in terrific shape!"

Arthur was changing from his golf clothes when Leda returned home. "Arthur, come downstairs, it is time for a drink before dinner!" Leda's voice cut into the fog of his thoughts. *Later, there will be time to tell her later,* Arthur decided as he entered the living room. He picked up the mail on the side table and sat down.

Leda entered with a tray of Martinis, holding them at bay to avoid touching her white dress. "Here is the Leda specialty," she boomed. "I love the Dorothy Thompson saying, 'I love martinis, two at the most, three, I am under the table, four I am under the host.' However, since I have already been under the host, I think one Martini before dinner will be adequate." Arthur and Leda roared with laughter. Leda, with a Martini in one hand and Arthur's pictures of Montana in the other, sat down.

Arthur asked her, "And what is new around here?"

"Yesterday I had a call from my nephew, Frank, who said his wife is expecting their second child."

"Great news, Leda, you can be a Great-Aunt again."

A Great-Aunt, terrific! I feel pushed into the rubbish heap of humanity. Why do people so rejoice at birth? I know I should be pleased but it is the easiest of human functions. It requires no education, no training, and no prerequisites. It requires, only an activity equal in complexity to a fart.

"The human fetus is the world's most perfect example of a parasite." Leda said to an astonished Arthur. "I have told you many times that when I was nine I reached the conclusion that the only reason people have children is to fulfill the dreams of the parents. Will this child be an improvement over my nephew? "

Arthur lit another cigarette and decided not to pursue her train of thought.

Leda loved the scent of tobacco. "Arthur, you realize that smoking is despised but will probably come into fashion again since nicotine has many advantages. It will make people die younger, which will be perceived as a great good when the majority of the population will be old, with a life expectancy of one hundred twenty, in nursing homes slowly dying of dementias."

Arthur put out his cigarette and said after some thought, "Yes, the future will be very different. Not only will there be a surfeit of seniors but also intermarriage among all races will equalize, pacify, homogenize, and level out all differences. A time will come when everyone will be café au lait with genetically dominant brown eyes and the blonde, blue-eyed people of the world will disappear."

In the dining room a formal table had red, fragrant roses in an artfully arranged centerpiece, the silver was heavy and glistening, the plates were Limoges. Leda poured red wine into the Baccarat crystal goblets. Arthur said with relish, "This combination of smoked fishes with a green sauce is delicious."

"Of course it is good, you eat anything. I presume you even eat bugs and toads on those long treks through the Montana wilderness." A perfectly cooked lemon chicken with rice and artichokes followed. Raspberries ended the meal due to their calorie count. The conversation turned to Arthur's career and the frantic calls from his office during his time away. But then Leda thought it was too late to launch into a deep discussion of politics.

After dinner, Leda took a bath soaking in water scented with Ysatis. She toweled off and looked at her reflection in the mirrored walls. *Some mirrors are friendly, the backlit ones, where they reflect my ideal vision of me. The unfriendly mirrors, usually on city streets in harsh sunlight reveal a hideous stranger. Yes, mirrors have a lot of power. Did not the ancients fear them because they were thought to steal your soul? But they give me my soul, they give me myself; after all, how else would I know who I was if not for the mirrors? They also give me company since in a room with mirrors, I am never alone- I always have myself.*

Turning back her bed she felt the 900 thread Egyptian cotton sheets and stroked their softness. One of the greatest comforts of a third of our life is a luxurious bed. Her dreams took her again into the desert and she felt the dry stinging sands whirling about her even as she lay in silken splendor. Arthur was beside her and life was perfect. What more could she want? What soundless scream impelled her to want change?

♦

Arthur could not fall asleep. In seeing Leda running toward him at the airport, he saw her running away from time, from life. There was always something about her that was incapable of understanding reality. The reality of life being as it is, the reality of becoming older, of acceptance, of limitations and especially the reality of the human need to continue the life process. She wanted perfection from life, from him and, most of all, from herself. Her weight was sacred and a few pound variation led to a week of lettuce, egg whites, and accompanying bad humor. Leda was a strain, a constant taskmaster; disappointed when he was just himself. She was a ruthless censor of his attire. Arthur bought a beret in Paris and Leda did not care for it, "It makes you look like an unsuccessful artist". The beret went missing. She always expected more from him and sometimes he felt crushed by the pressure. He had been attracted to her by her intellect, breadth of interests and original thinking. She was a beautiful woman but it was her original mind that seduced him.

The week in Montana without her was necessary. He had to make the trip alone in order to think, to plan. The last visit with his doctor was kept in strictest confidence. It was a secret that he was almost keeping from himself. Mortality at 70 should not be a surprise, but it always is.

Perhaps he had made a mistake in the major question of marriage to Leda. But can there be mistakes in life? A decision is made only on partial facts since we do not know the future. So at the time is a decision was made, obviously, it was the right decision. No one would decide against their own best interests. He was physically attracted to Leda but he did not envision the strain of her critical nature. And if he had known of the energy it would take to cope with her would he have married her? But he did not know at the time so how could it have been a mistake?

After a restless night Arthur was interrupted by the sunlight of a new day. *Today, I will have to talk with Leda about my future.* He reached over and stroked Leda's face waking her with "Good Morning, darling" as she rose and yawned.

Arthur looked at Leda, sitting on the side of the bed with the strong sun streaming and realized that she was a woman approaching old age. Her sheer black nightgown revealed some thickening at the waist and the start of a belly. As she looked down to reach her slippers, her neck showed visible wrinkles. He knew that his wife strived for perfection in their marriage but it gave him the premonition that someday all would explode. How could she hold in a bland, superficial existence when she was searching for excitement and truth, for something profound? He knew it was a matter of time before he would have to let her go into the dangerous minefield of reality. She looked so vulnerable, so fragile, how could he burden her with more sorrow at this time? Perhaps his news could wait.

CHAPTER 3

Leda, in her red robe, joined Arthur at the sunlit breakfast table and hesitantly said; "I didn't bring this up before because I didn't want to overwhelm you. While you were gone I had several long conversations with Aliyah, my classmate in medical school. She wants me to come to Syria to help her with Palestinian refugees. She said she would arrange it." Her excitement was palpable in her flushed face and shining eyes.

Arthur put down his *Wall Street Journal*. "I know the Palestinian situation outrages your sense of fairness. You tell everyone Palestine was a Jewish Kingdom only in 1250 BC and was not considered a Jewish state again until 1948 when 750,000 Palestinians were evicted. So now you want to help the world's underdog and correct the injustice of 70 years. This is your sacred mission. Is it because you missed all the politics of Viet Nam while you were too busy studying medicine?"

"I really want to do this. I must do this. It would be my stand for justice."

Arthur was amused with the idea of his wife becoming a political activist. *This desire to have justice in the world must be her latest fad following skiing, painting, opera and tennis,* thought Arthur smiled as he again perused *The Wall Street Journal* with diligent attention to his stock portfolio.

"Arthur, this is not a joke."

"I still can't believe you are that serious. What is this? Doctors Without Borders? Amnesty International?" Arthur asked as he picked up his coffee.

Leda resumed eating her cereal. "Actually, Aliyah tells me that all of these organizations are so bogged down with red tape that it becomes almost impossible to get to the Palestinians," she said with real concern.

"What are you, an anti-Semite? You will become a pariah like President Carter," said an astonished Arthur. "I know you are bothered by the conflict but you know suicide bombers have inflicted a lot of damage on the innocent in Israel. Why, I was discussing this with a friend I made in Montana who is Jewish and he would be horrified at your one-sidedness," concluded Arthur.

"I know there is a just cause to the Israeli side, but the unfairness consists of the fact that Israel has America to care for it in terms of the press, public opinion, money, money, money and arms. Whereas who gives a damn for the Palestinians – not even their Arab brothers. No, they need help and I want to help because they are the neediest. I will not ignore my conscience!" Leda stated with passion. She hit the table with such emphasis that even Frodo started to bark.

Arthur stood up, "Leda, have you simply lost all your

marbles? Is this a late-life crisis? Put this away for now, we will discuss this later when you have had time to think this through. I have to get to the office."

He put papers in his briefcase and was almost out the door when Leda rushed to him, hugged him, and said, "We have tickets for this evening's reception for Vice-President Chester at the Conservative Club." His expression showed his degree of unhappiness with this news. *Another fundraiser— more lies crafted to extract money, more amorphous speeches signifying nothing.* The car came for Arthur to whisk him away to Manhattan and they made arrangements to meet at the Club.

"Don't be late," chided Leda, "You know I hate the cocktail hour without you."

That evening, Leda sensed the dichotomy between the pleasure she was having in reviewing her formal wear, choosing her jewelry and her stated goal of becoming a saint to help the poor Palestinians. In Alberta Ferretti floor-length black velvet she admired her size six figure. Manolo Blahnik strappy diamante sandals completed her attire. A spray of Eau Du Soir perfume, and her Judith Leiber bag, and she was ready.

The Conservative club was a Manhattan fixture of old money. Black secret service limousines surrounded the club, due to the prominence of its guest of honor. She dropped her car with the valet parking service and joined the well-dressed throngs on the way to the Library. This room with its high ceilings and portraits of American presidents and their wives

17

was the cocktail venue. She had just started a conversation with a couple she knew when she saw Arthur in his tuxedo waving to her at the entrance.

As Arthur joined her, they went off to the bar for drinks. In the crowd, Leda teetered for a second on her four-inch heels and backed into a woman. "I am so, so sorry, Mrs. Chester. I did not mean to injure my favorite author of mystery books. I truly thought the last one; *The Dead White House Mistress* was brilliant."

"No harm done. Are you an officer of this club?"

"My name is Dr. Leda Eimont and I am only a member." Mrs. Chester asked if Leda knew her personal physician and launched into description of her latest visit. The noise was at a three-drink level but it did not stop a discussion of medical problems with a captive physician.

By the time Arthur came around, weaving through the cocktail crowds bringing Martinis, the women had developed a bond. "Please call me Amy," said Mrs. Chester and Leda found herself the recipient of a card with Amy's private number. "Call me. I would love to have lunch with you."

The dinner in the high two-storied ballroom reflected the candle-illuminated guests in a profusion of mirrors. Tables in white and gold with a wealth of white roses provided the setting for a dinner of smoked salmon, filet mignon and chocolate cake, Vice-President Chester launched into a vitriolic speech calling for war in the Middle East to protect our way of life.

"It is a proven fact that Saddam Hussein has Weapons of Mass Destruction. Not only is he a murderer of his own people but also a megalomaniac who wants to rule the entire

Middle East. The State of Israel, our only ally, our dearest friend would be the first victim in Saddam's march toward nuclear hegemony. We already lost the Trade Towers and 3000 of our brave American citizens, but if Saddam is not stopped next time it will be entire American cities. We must preserve our way of life in the face of people who hate us, who hate democracy and freedom..."

Leda could not follow the reasoning. *If we are to punish Saddam Hussein for having nuclear weapons, why not punish North Korea or Israel for that matter? There was no way in hell Iraq was a danger to the United States.*

Leda went back to the bar for another drink to ease her anger when she found herself standing next to a tall handsome man. "After you," he said smiling.

"I need a drink after that speech" replied Leda introducing herself and holding out her hand.

"Richard Attenborough." He said with a smile and a squeeze to her hand.

"Are you perhaps with the Chester group?" Leda inquired.

"I'm with the United Nations High Commission on Refugees and I am a new member here."

"I'm so happy to meet you. I have an overwhelming personal interest in the Palestinian refugee situation. I am planning to go to the Middle East to try to help. What is your take on the current situation?"

Dear Dr. Eimont," Attenborough said in a whisper as he looked around, "the Palestinian refugee situation is the only one that we at the UN are not allowed to discuss. It is considered too controversial for the United States and we all toe the line. I am personally very sorry, but as long as America holds the dominant hand and it feels that any discussion would throw prejudice on Israel, our hands are tied."

Leda felt crushed. Was there a complete absence of truth and justice? *Did the world ignore the Jewish people in World War II just as they were now doing to the Palestinians?* She walked back to her table as the Vice-President was finishing his speech with, "It is our primary duty to protect Israel, our special friend, from her hostile neighbors." to resounding applause. Helplessness flooded her before she realized that she absolutely must do something about this injustice. A flurry of cards exchanged, kisses blown into the air, pictures taken before the trip home.

Arthur was having a nightcap of scotch when Leda approached him in the den. "Arthur, you know how upset I was tonight listening to that speech," said Leda sitting down and removing her sparkling high heels.

"How can intelligent, educated people that were at that dinner tonight listen to this fantasy, to these lies? How can they suspend their logic to agree with the premise that the Muslim world hates us? And the basis for this hatred is because we are a democracy?" Leda sneered and stood up. "Why could he not say that war is necessary because of oil and Israel? If we want more oil why not invade Canada where we get 22% of our oil. We could quickly conquer their 20 million people and we would get all the benefit of their territory and natural resources. As far as Israel goes it is a foreign country. Despite all the lobbies it is not the 51st state of the United States."

"My God! You know we lost our last war with Canada! Only you would have thought of that scenario." Arthur chuckled. "Of course I know. The government is not acting in the best interests of America any longer. The United States has no vital interests in Iraq. The last thing in the world that we need is a war in the Middle East with a country that poses no threat to us whatsoever. The risks of this adventure are enormous. It will turn the entire Muslim world against us and wreck the world economy."

"Arthur, my plans are non-negotiable. My mind is made up so that I don't think I could be swayed. Since I have sold my practice I have been looking for something to occupy my energies. I have discarded the idea of teaching. I don't have the time left in my life to pound the basics into the students of today," Leda said as she removed her jewelry. "I've reached a decision that I cannot just talk and complain about the Palestinian situation. I must do something about it. " Leda said with conviction.

Arthur was silently sipping his scotch with a look of sadness.

Leda, looking away from Arthur, continued, "I spoke with Aliyah this morning and told her I am coming to Damascus."

Arthur's face was so devoid of expression Leda thought he did not hear her.

"Arthur, this is as necessary to me as the air I breathe." Failing to get a reaction from Arthur, Leda went upstairs to the bedroom and as she brushed her teeth she noticed her tears. *What is this madness?* In a few minutes she was aware that Arthur had entered the bedroom.

"I will be ordering my tickets for my flight in the morning. Since I don't know how things will go I will get an open return date," Leda said as she got into bed. "I would like to leave in a few weeks."

"Do you have any idea what you are doing?" asked Arthur tonelessly as if her actions were outside the perimeter of his life.

"I know this is something that cannot wait. I have never in my life taken a stand or believed in anything strongly enough to take a risk. If I don't do this now, I may as well give up on the rest of my life. It will have stood for nothing."

Leda was crying and her features did not improve screwed up in sorrow. Arthur, seeing her so distraught, sat down on the bed and took her in his arms. "Leda, we must talk this through. This is not a holiday at a spa. There is danger here in a potential clash of civilizations between Islam and the West." Arthur continued with his voice full of concern, "Not only will you be in physical danger, but this action of yours could also put you on the blacklist with the United States government. You will be considered a terrorist sympathizer and God only knows how that could affect our lives. After all, this is not just a holiday where you can return to life as usual. There are grave consequences. Look at Jimmy Walker who fought with the Taliban."

"But Arthur, I am not going over there to fight. I abhor violence. I want to go there to help people."

You are a woman! Are you going to put on the veils and try to pass for a Muslim? What kind of help do you want to give? As for Aliyah, how well do you know her? She could be connected to some terrorist group." Arthur said with anger.

After a pause with a deep sigh he looked sadly at her and said, "How long will you be gone?" He knew the die was cast.

Leda looked at him in shock, "Arthur, you realize I am not kidding."

"Of course you're not kidding. That's the problem. You probably feel it is your destiny to throw yourself into this fire. You will never win, darling. You must not be naïve. There are forces on both sides that are in it just for themselves. You will learn, Leda, that the world is very grey and there is evil everywhere."

Leda knew that of all the things she was sacrificing, time with Arthur was the biggest loss. Functioning without him would be her most difficult challenge. "I plan to be home in three months. I know this seems stupid and reckless but I could not live with myself if I did not follow my conscience."

Arthur took her in his arms and kissed her forehead "I always suspected that a part of you wanted to be a saint, ever since you told me of running away to the convent in high school. I'm your husband, not your jailer. I couldn't live with your constant recriminations. Just make sure you keep in touch with me constantly and with the American Embassy. And leave at the first sign of trouble. That's not too much to ask, is it?"

The door opened and Leda stepped into her future.

CHAPTER 4

Loss is a fact of life but some losses are harder than others. The loss of Leda at this time would be catastrophic. Arthur wanted to share his diagnosis with Leda but the timing was wrong. If I told her my problem she would not go. *Maybe I will still be in remission long enough for Leda to return. Or even better, my death could be so sudden that Leda would be spared the torture of watching me suffer.* Leda did not believe in weakness and any discussion of illness was always followed by an omniscient prescription to health. How could he possibly discuss this fatal condition with Leda? She would bombard him with solutions when he just wanted warmth, understanding and sympathy.

Arthur finished the call with his broker regarding some options on commodities. He had placed a large bet on grain and loved the excitement of the gamble. *All of life is a gamble.* Surveying the view from his window on Wall Street, Manhattan was spread out in front of him and the East River was reflected in the mirrored windows of the adjacent building. The corporation was doing very well and he considered some successful acquisitions. He had two competent candidates who could assume his position and wanted to tie up any loose ends. He knew his energy was fading like sand running through his fingers. Soon he would be unable to continue. Heaviness and sadness seared his soul since Leda told him of her plans. He had a premonition that this decision of hers would not just be a fruitful, altruistic stint in a foreign country.

He answered his phone calls, signed some memos and told his secretary to call his car. He wanted to leave for home.

Leda, exhausted and drained, came home after approaching drug companies and her colleagues for donations of drugs and medical instruments. Considering a salad, salmon and spinach for dinner, she decided on a very cold Sauvignon Blanc as she walked into the living room. Arthur was sitting there in the dark. A sharp pain entered her heart. She had made her decision to leave him, to desert him, and seeing him so bereft stung her conscience.

"Arthur, should we have dinner?" Arthur did not reply.

"Rough day?" Leda asked as Arthur stood up slowly and moved toward the bar.

"Let's have a drink first; I feel I really need one after today."

After several drinks Leda was shocked to see Arthur crying. "Leda, have you really considered what you are doing? Are you that unhappy with me?"

Leda took him in her arms, "It will be all right, you will see, it will be all right." She had never seen him so vulnerable and it frightened her. She had only observed tears at his father's death. *What was she doing to so upset the balance of things?*

After dinner Arthur went to sleep early and Leda continued reading *Nunquam*, a novel by Lawrence Durrell:

> *"Quick, let us make love before another human being is born. More and more people, Benedicta, the world is overflowing; but the quality is going down correspondingly. There is no point in just people – nothing multiplied by nothing is still nothing.*

Leda put the book down and thought of death. Her mother's death revealed life's futility and destroyed all she believed in. She dissected events looking for some clue, some evidence that her mother's death had some meaning, some message. Elizabeth Eimont received a great blow with the diagnosis of macular degeneration. Although she would never be blind, it would destroy her favorite hobby, reading. Leda, the ophthalmologist, was helpless with this incurable disease and tried to compensate by buying her a diamond ring.

"Look at the diamond, mama, and each time you look at it remember how much I love you," Leda offered.

"Dear, I hope that the diamond does not come from your life like a solidified tear." Elizabeth could never understand Leda's childlessness.

The first sign of the insidious disease was a frugal repast, -a salad and some bread. Opening the refrigerator later for a glass of milk, she saw her favorite beef stew and apple pie. She smiled - Mama must have forgotten. Then her mother's friends complained that she was starting to ignore them. "You must realize," Leda explained, "that she cannot see well anymore, so please be patient with her and approach her closely and give her your name." Then the calls started about missing items. Leda reassured her mother that it was because of her vision.

Months later, a call from her father at a Florida hospital sent her to the airport to fly stand-by. At her bedside, she saw her mother who gave her a beautiful smile. Her distraught father seemed helpless. "What happened?" demanded Leda.

"I drank something by mistake," replied her mother. Leda looked with sorrow at her helpless mother who had been an example of strength. She had been a neurosurgeon at a time of few female physicians in the country.

She went to find Dr. Shore, handsome and indifferent, who explained that her mother had ingested a bottle of laundry stain remover and needed to have her stomach pumped.

"She has vision problems and probably mistook it for mouthwash."

"No," Dr. Shore replied, "It is not that simple. After running tests to exclude all other conditions, I came to the conclusion that it is Alzheimer's disease."

Leda gasped in shock "I had no idea. What is the prognosis?"

"You are a physician so you must know," pontificated Dr. Shore by rote, "As the brain forms it develops layers with increasingly sophisticated functions. Recognition, speech, walking, and toilet training follow in sequence in a progressive evolution. Apparently, in Alzheimer's, the brain gets destroyed in the inverse manner. First, there will be the destruction of the higher functions of reasoning and logic, then a loss speech, of walking, and control of bodily functions until at last there will be a helpless infant left. And when swallowing and breathing stop, it will end. However, this slow torture can last up to 10 years. I am sorry to be the bearer of such bad news."

Leda had given many patients a horrific diagnosis in her years in medicine, but she had never realized what it felt like on the receiving end. She did not realize that the precise textbook rendering of the disease did not take into account the victim and caregivers who could only emotionally envision the disease. There was no safety net provided, no cushion of warmth, no understanding in this recital of information. She understood the full devastation of the news.

There were four years of round the clock private nurses, two broken hips, infections, and deteriorating bodily conditions. There were also moments of astounding lucidity when her mother thanked her for her care.

At the end Leda expected Elizabeth to fall into eternal sleep in her arms. But Elizabeth woke with a start and for three hours struggled against death. Leda gave her more morphine, more medicine, but the sounds of drowning continued. She was a doctor, but at the moment when it mattered most, she was helpless. In desperation, she called 911. Reaching the hospital in a driving Florida rain, she was informed that her mother had died. So, the last minutes that she had looked forward to—a peaceful and loving farewell—never materialized. Kneeling by her mother's body trying to pray, to accept, *Christ, you only suffered for three days before your death – try four years!*

After her mother's death, trying to find solace, she met Father Delos, a blond, handsome and brilliant Catholic priest, at her favorite Italian restaurant in Manhattan. She had read his books on theology, met him, and developed a friendship. She described her mother's illness as Father Delos rubbed his forehead and listened. Leda took a sip of scotch and speared her shrimp scampi.

"Father, is the earth more crowded, as I get older? Was I the only one in the universe at one time? I was so special as a child and so inconsequential now—just one speck of dust among the teeming billions."

"All children have themselves at the center of the universe. With maturity it is normal to perceive the rest of humanity. You are a Catholic. You are not inconsequential to God."

"And what about life after death? Would two and a half billion be good and the remainder bad? Would a team of angels do the celestial bookkeeping and separate them? Maybe the good numbers would be much smaller: perhaps only true believers need apply. And who would these be? The Greek Orthodox under the Prelate of Antioch? The Alewite sect of the Shiites of Islam? The members of the Latter Day Saints led by the Angel Moroni? All the Roman Catholics led by members of Opus Dei?"

"Christ came on earth to establish the true religion and you well know that the only religion to have a succession from Peter is the one, holy, Catholic church."

"How does this work? Was God a racist when he declared

His chosen people? Or were there different Gods for different people? Do you not speculate on this father?"

"You think too much and you analyze too much. We must have Faith which never answers to reason." He let her vent but hoped to change the subject.

But Leda had a torrent to leash out. "Could I have followed to perfection the wrong rulebook? And then what? An eternity of suffering? Worse than what I had here? Or will everyone participate in the feast of eternity, an everlasting love-in where all is truly forgiven for everyone? And if so, and God is really all that good, why the misery and pain and injustice now? Did He construct all this as a cosmic joke?"

Father Delos had no reply as he finished his osso bucco.

Leda ate her last shrimp and continued, "The open door policy for eternity makes far more sense; after all, no one sets out to do evil. All evil has some purpose and justification in the mind of the evildoer. Even Hitler and Stalin and Mao had their own rationale."

Father Delos sat in silence and contemplation. "Hubris is a great sin. Leda, do not make a complicated issue out of the fact that you were born a Catholic to love God and your neighbor. Do not be confounded by complexity. To know all is to be God and that is why Adam and Eve lost paradise."

"Why did God give me a mind to question if I am to accept all?" They ordered coffee and Tiramisu. Thinking about death required a countervailing sweetness.

"Sudden death is preferable my mother's fate. To be helpless, dependent, and a burden is unacceptable to me. I hate to admit to any weakness much less to be dependent for complete care of my bodily functions. To know the progression and foresee the end after years of subhuman existence and suffering! Assisted suicide at diagnosis is the answer. But what about eternal life? Father, help me understand."

Father Delos shifted in his seat, furrowed his brow, and said in an authoritative voice, "God gives life and He takes it away."

"Father, how can we not help end these hopeless cases? You put your beloved crippled dog to sleep and my father shot his favorite horse when he broke a leg. It is only out of love and avoidance of suffering that we act in this manner. How much more do people suffer, and yet we stand aside as if to imply, go ahead and suffer!"

"Leda, dear Leda, God is good. It is in His hands," argued Father Delos. "Suicide is unnatural. Because people have an eternal soul they must obey the natural law. Only God chooses the end of life and man must not interfere."

"No! If that were the case, the Church would be against heart transplants since it is unnatural to prolong life by the artificial means of a mechanical heart or a heart transplant. If the heart God gave you is failing, what right does man have to replace it? And if people cannot participate morally in the end of life, what about the travesty at its beginning, with test tube babies and surrogate mothers? Is that also not unnatural? If we can manipulate the beginning of life for the happiness of mankind, could we not also manipulate the end?"

Leda had another scotch as Father Delos said, "This is a very complicated issue." There were no answers here she realized. Perhaps she would find them in Damascus.

CHAPTER 5

Leda, clutching her Air France ticket, left Arthur at the gate. Tears welled up from grief and indecision. A strong impulse pulled her to run into his arms and forget the outside world. She wanted to stroke his thick, grey hair and look into his aquamarine eyes. She may not be able to do much about justice in the Middle East, and perhaps ruin her life and marriage. But she had to go as if by the force of a mutant gene that conquered her. If a cancer can be latent for many years before expressing itself, why not fulminating life desires? It is important to honor a marriage but it is more important to honor yourself. She turned again, but Arthur was gone.

She found herself sitting next to a woman with a baby on the flight to Paris. The moment after takeoff she asked the stewardess for another seat, took a sleeping pill, and sank into oblivion. Flying, to Leda, was to be packed in a can of sardines getting hurtled through space.

De Gaulle Airport was a familiar place. Leda had enough time before her connecting flight to eat escargot at the airport

Brasserie since she missed the Air France dinner. Visiting the duty-free cosmetics counter, she experienced the tranquilizing effects of shopping. The Air France flight to Damascus was not crowded and there were people with a decidedly Middle Eastern look. Three women wore the traditional Arabic dress, the kaffiyeh and djellaba. Several of the men wore the red and white or black and white headscarves with black bands. Leda, wearing an olive green jumpsuit, most comfortable for travel, decided that the woman sitting next to her would not intrude upon her privacy. She looked at her last e-mail from Aliyah.

> *Dearest Leda,*
>
> *You will be here tomorrow! Your room has a view overlooking the mountains. My medical practice is to be taken over by a good friend, Talib, who has recently taken a sabbatical from teaching. We are to work in a clinic for Palestinian refugees in a very poor section. I am so happy you are coming, so together we will make some progress. You will see for yourself what a desperate situation we have. I hope you are bringing antibiotics and vitamins for the children, as many have severe malnutrition. I will meet your Air France flight with great joy.*
>
> *Fondly, Aliya*

In medical school when she first saw Aliyah dressed in black with a silk kaffiyeh Leda took her for a Catholic nun.

Aliyah with her clothes and British accent stood out among the five female medical students. At the beginning, she was so quiet with a desperate wish to blend into the background, that the slightest movement towards her made her jump like a frightened rabbit. Leda was drawn to her by a need protect this shivering creature with the dark liquid eyes. Aliyah's brilliance made her a wonderful study companion and the two girls discovered that they had very much in common. They both subscribed to the same taste in music, a love of silence and great interest in world affairs.

Aliyah lived in Professor Ahmed's home in a small private suite on the top floor of his old Victorian. He taught Middle Eastern History at the university and his family was considered suitable to protect Aliyah from Western influences during her studies. The Professor was a heavy-set man with a scraggly beard and small, deep-set eyes that burned brightly with intelligence. His hair was unruly and it seemed as if his clothes were always trying to get away from the torture of belonging to him. His shirts had a way of escaping his trousers and he was constantly pushing the tails back in. His shoelaces were always coming undone and even his jackets seemed to be forever slipping off his shoulders. Aliyah would laugh and say that it was just because his body was not used to Western dress and he belonged in a djellaba.

His enormous house in Hyde Park was a raucous palace of a myriad of interests shared by his five children. They knew no discipline and his sweet saint of a wife spent her days in futile endeavor in establishing some sense of order. The children, ranging from 6 to 18 were a terror to behold with all their projects. At any time Leda entered to visit Aliyah, she would see a bushel of leaves for a botany project, test tubes set up in the kitchen for a chemistry experiment, a dozen creepy-crawlies for a nature study, a trampoline for gymnastic practice, and some violin music trying to rise up above the din. Leda could not imagine a household with so much activity; much less imagine her Aliyah living in this atmosphere.

It was from Aliyah that Leda first became aware of the Middle East and its problems in a very personal sense. One time at dinner Leda said, "Pass the water," the professor, filling her glass said, "A big problem is the theft of Palestinian water by Israel. They sell it back to the Palestinians at an enormous profit." The dinners avoided alcohol and pork, "Islam has its prohibitions." Professor Ahmed explained Palestinian history in detail "Seventeen civilizations occupied the land of Palestine which many feel was the cradle of civilization."

"Why there?"

"It was at the crossroads of many peoples and many cultures. The Jewish people never forgot their covenant with God that they owned the land."

They all watched the movie *Lawrence of Arabia*. Leda was very moved.

"The British utilized Lawrence to organize the Arabs to fight the Turks, allied to the Germans in World War I. In return for their help in defeating the Axis powers the Arabs were offered independence from the Ottoman Empire. But there was a great betrayal. There was a secret agreement called Picot-Sykes where the French and British carved up the old Ottoman Empire for themselves and there was no partition for the Arabs or the Jewish people."

35

"Why did not the British keep their promise to the Arabs?"

"They wanted the land for themselves."

"How did the Jews get their land?"

"The Zionists were very powerful and wealthy in Britain and they promised the British financial help in the war if they let a small part of Palestine become a Jewish homeland."

"They gave away what was not theirs to give!" Leda

A heady world was exposed—a completely mysterious, mystical, foreign place- she welcomed with open arms. It seemed that the whole turbulent, sand-filled Middle East was her Shangri-La. Leda started dreaming of Bedouin tents, camels, pyramids and Arabian princes— as an antidote to the daily grind of life in medical school filled with competition, sickness, and the smell of formaldehyde.

In the Six-Day War, Leda first learned about Aliyah's despair. She told Leda that her family was originally from Palestine and her suffering during the war was acute. Aliyah received letters from her family and her expressive, dark eyes with their phenomenally long lashes had a haunted look. In all the spare moments her studies would allow, Leda read about the history of the Middle East and was more and more dismayed at the ignorance of most Americans about this region. The Ottoman Empire and World War I and II became her subjects as she delved into these areas as a reward for having learned the microscopic anatomy of the liver or the etiology of Lupus or the treatment of adenocarcinoma.

After graduation, Aliyah accepted an internship and earned a subsequent Ph.D. at Mass General in conjunction with Harvard. Leda stayed on at Chicago, delving into ophthalmology. Aliyah became a neonatal heart surgeon with a Ph.D. in physiology. Her intention was always to return to Syria, so Leda was not surprised when Aliyah went back in spite of a flurry of lucrative offers from the best neonatal practices in the country. "I must help my people," was her response.

When Aliyah married a Syrian physician, Abdullah, Leda had her Board exams and could not come to the wedding. Leda had met him on one of his visits to Professor Ahmed's family in Chicago. Abdullah was a few years younger than Aliyah and a complete foil for Aliyah's serious nature. He was a jokester—a lively, wiry fellow who was a constant hurricane around the calm eye of Aliyah. His flashing white teeth and broad smile with his outrageous comments would pull Aliyah outside of herself and she would smile shyly at this dervish of a man. Leda could not understand Aliyah's attraction to Abdullah—*whatever made them marry? Beautiful, solemn, intellectual Aliyah with this comedian? Their families knew one another and pronounced them suitable, but how could such a clown ever hope to understand the deep soul of Aliyah?*

A few months after the wedding, Aliyah said she could not imagine greater happiness but pregnancy made her ecstatic. Leda promised to come to meet the new family in Damascus. The child, Deya, was born with a congenital heart defect and died during surgery in spite of all of Aliyah's efforts as part of a neonatal surgical team. The irony of being a neo-natal heart surgeon and not being able to save her own child devastated her. She stopped her surgical practice in Damascus, started a general pediatric practice, and never had any more children. After the baby's death, Abdullah was Aliyah's salvation since he was the only one who could pull her out of her grief and make her smile. *Sometimes it is hard to predict logically what our deepest needs would be and our instincts sometimes prophesy the future.*

The phone call sixteen years ago came from a voice Leda could not recognize. "Leda, Abdullah died this morning." The pain in Aliyah's voice was palpable through the thousands of miles. "He was feeling weak and I hospitalized him on Thursday. On Friday, he was kidding me about pretending to be sick to avoid his least favorite patient, a demanding hypochondriac. We were running all the known tests but not coming up with any definitive results. Last night, he was about to be released but I insisted we wait for this morning. He died just before daybreak. At autopsy, the cause of death was an abdominal aneurysm."

"Aliyah, I will come."

"Thank you, but there is no need. In accordance with Islamic customs, he will be buried within 24 hours, so by the time you arrive in Damascus it will be all over. I need to be by myself. You must come to Syria someday, but not under these circumstances."

A flight attendant distributing landing cards stopped Leda's flow of memories. The flight crew was preparing for landing and Leda felt the excitement of finally being able to see Aliyah on her home ground. She had described this city and her way of life so often, but Leda still could not imagine the reality of the ancient architecture and exotic lifestyle. She felt some disappointment that Abdullah with his insane sense of humor would not be playing some joke on her at the arrivals lounge. *Abdullah would have always been the young trickster looking for ways to turn the rational world upside down.*

My world has turned upside down by this irresistible propulsion. Arthur knows that, he understands. He is my anchor, my safe harbor no matter what I encounter here.

CHAPTER 6

Leda did not see Aliyah in a swirl of humanity. Finally, a small, veiled woman clothed in black came up to her. "Leda," she said. Leda had not seen Aliyah in many years, and some snapshots did not adequately show what had transpired. She seemed so fragile, so shrunken, and there was an aroma of mustiness about her. Leda tried not to show her shock. In her mind, Aliyah was still the young, classical beauty of years ago. The death of Abdullah must have shriveled her body and ground up her soul.

"Leda, you haven't changed! You look just like when we were in school!" Aliyah said as a servant picked up her baggage. Leda wanted to say something in return but could not give empty compliments and was glad of the distraction of moving through the crowds to the car to avoid a reply.

The narrow city streets presaged an ancient city, Damascus, the oldest city in the world. People in all sorts of colorful garb, as well as vendors with carts of fruits, vegetables, flyspecked meats, donkey carts, and taxis filled the streets. As a chicken got out of the way of their rapidly moving black limousine, Leda imagined the numbers of accidents in such haphazard traffic. They left the city proper and wound up on a potholed road climbing the hills surrounding the city. Cypress trees lined the road and the air took on a fresher aspect. They arrived at a large iron gate surrounded by a stone wall.

"This is home, Leda. I have always wanted you to see it. The stone wall was a part of the ancient city wall and my grandfather, in government at the time, just requisitioned the wall to be moved to surround his estate."

"Beautiful wall" said Leda. *So much for the accuracy of historical monuments. Since so much of life was in constant flux, the preservation of the past, in stone or memory, was hopeless.*

The cool entry hall was a relief after the hazardous drive and there were profuse apologies from the chauffeur for the broken air-conditioner. "You see, it is very difficult to get parts for German cars and also there is a problem with theft," he said in perfect English. The little man was toothless and bald and it was a mystery to Leda where he learned his English, but fatigue was starting to overcome her curiosity and when Aliyah led her to a large, corner room with crosswind breezes. Leda stretched out on the soft sheets and went to sleep.

The fire of the setting sun through the gauze-veiled windows startled Leda into wakefulness. For a moment, she was disoriented and then looked at her wrinkled suit and realized she had not undressed. The connecting private bathroom had no shower so she filled a bathtub with tepid water and luxuriated in the salts that were placed on the ledge. The aroma of jasmine was relaxing and the salts left her skin soft and silky. She unpacked her suitcases and the practiced habit of adorning her face was accomplished even in the poor light. She dressed with care putting on a long, loose dress of blue and gold with gold sandals. Moving aside the sheer curtains, she looked out over the gardens filled with fruit trees and cypress. The estate was much larger and more impressive than Aliyah had led her to believe. Descending the staircase, she saw Aliyah, completely changed, wearing slacks and a blouse straight from the pages of Vogue. She laughed at the dichotomy. "Aliyah, you look like a tourist, and I, the native."

Leda toured the rest of the house with its large, high-ceilinged rooms and heavy dark, carved furniture. The most beautiful aspects were the highly polished floors with a myriad of Persian carpets. In sharp contrast, there were no decorations on the stark, white walls. Leda's high-heeled sandals caught one of the silken carpet strands just at the entry into the dining room and she found herself on the verge of falling when two strong hands grabbed her by the waist and averted disaster. The aroma of eucalyptus was evident as she turned and a man smiled at her. "Leda, I want you to meet Talib. He is to run my clinic when we go to the Palestinian refugee camp," Aliyah explained with a wistful look.

Leda thanked him for his rescue as she examined him. He seemed to be in his forties, very tall and slender with jet black hair. His elongated face, a potential model for a Modigliani, was in proportion with a beautiful full mouth and very white teeth. His eyes looked sad, as if centuries of tragedy were buried in his brown irises. Leda had to catch her breath at the absolute perfection of this man.

The table already held other people and they were so rapidly introduced that Leda could only understand that there was a sister and brother of Aliyah's with their spouses and some neighbors. "So you are a physician?" Leda inquired as she was seated next to Talib.

"Yes, officially I am Talib al-Zawahiri, Professor of Neurosurgery at the University of Cairo. But I took a sabbatical in Damascus. I am writing a book about a new technique in neurosurgery that I developed," answered Talib staring at her intently.

Leda answered with a smile and a lilting voice, "You look far too young to have been a colleague of Abdullah's."

"I was a student of Abdullah's and I still am saddened by his untimely death. I do all I can for Aliyah because Abdullah was like a brother and a father to me." He never moved his piercing gaze from Leda.

Talib was drinking the sweet water at the table. Aliyah had offered an alcoholic drink to Leda but she knew that Muslims do not drink alcohol and that it was only their fervent hospitality that allowed them to keep some alcohol on hand for visitors. "No, thank you Aliyah, while I am here I will follow the ways of Islam," said Leda, placing her hand over her wine glass as a servant with a carafe stood by her side.

"Certainly you jest. For a professional American woman with your liberated values to consider living like a Muslim woman, even for three months, it is inconceivable," stated Talib quizzically raising one eyebrow.

"You underestimate me, Dr. al-Zawahiri," said Leda with obvious flirtation in her voice. She did not notice the glance that Aliyah gave to the two of them; she was so mesmerized by the handsome young doctor from the opposite side of the world.

"Since you will be living as a Muslim for the next few months, perhaps you will allow me to show you some of the city and introduce you to some of our customs," Talib offered with a smile as Aliyah seemed to start to object but then sank back into her chair. Even Leda noticed this latest concern on her friend's face. *Was she jealous? Could she have designs on him herself? Am I stepping into a problem?*

Aromas wafting in from the kitchen heightened their appetites. The dinner of crispy, spicy roast lamb with rice, cucumbers, skewered tomatoes, eggplants, yogurt, and other unidentifiable vegetables, each prepared with a variety of condiments, was delicious. Fruits and honey with sugared candies followed. The conversation centered on Leda and Aliyah's days in medical school and stories about Professor Ahmed and his unruly children who all turned out to be physicians, professors, a nuclear scientist and even a Nobel Prize winner. The talk of Abdullah brought sadness into the evening as Aliyah tried to tell funny stories about his tricks and jokes, but she could not hide her pain.

In saying his farewell, Talib again offered to show Leda the city," It would be my pleasure to expose the beauty and mystery of Damascus to you. The city would frame your beauty and mystery. It would be a pleasing portrait to me and I would be delighted to be your guide."

"I am sure that Aliyah would be a better guide since she is a native and you are from Egypt." She could see the relief flood Aliyah's face and knew she did the right thing although their relationship was a mystery to her.

Returning to her room, she called Arthur to tell him about her trip. As she talked non-stop she noticed none of the usual comments and questions from him. She finally stopped talking and asked, "Are you still unhappy with me for going?"

"No, I am very happy for you." but remained strangely silent. "I love you, Leda," he said sadly. His tone of voice was not normal in the radar of people intimate for many years. *Something is wrong.* Leda looked at her watch. *Of course, it must be very late in Connecticut, the seven hour time difference made it four in the morning. He was tired.*

The next day Aliyah and Leda prepared with comfortable shoes and large hats went sightseeing. Aliyah in a formal voice said, "Damascus, now a city of 5 million, has a history starting in 5000 BC when it was settled by the Barada River. Each corner had an artifact of a different ancient era in the epicenter of Damascus, the Old City, surrounded by a Roman wall.

Leda was excited to see the Souq al-Hamadiyyeh, the main covered market. The old cobbled streets were filled with vendors, bright colors, exotic spicy smells and bustling crowds. The two women spent happy hours bargaining for yards of silk, gold earrings, and hand-woven scarves. Leda laughingly told Aliyah, "I will probably need the empty medical supply containers for my shopping to be shipped back home".

At the end of the market they came upon the Omayyad Mosque, a breathtaking example of Muslim architecture with its intricate, priceless mosaics and three original minarets. The stained glass windows were a masterpiece of geometric designs. A plaque, translated by Aliyah said it was built in 705 AD on the site of ancient temples and a Christian cathedral.

Leda removed her shoes and covered her head with a scarf. The vast mosque with a sea of Persian carpets and only an indication of the direction of Mecca lacked any paintings or statues. *It is hard to represent God, and the Muslims got it right by not attempting to put a face on God. Christians are exposed to paintings of the Child Jesus as a miniature adult, God as an angry old man, or the fires of hell with devils. Spiritual imagination is so much more powerful.* While they were in the mosque, the plaintive call of the minarets sounded and people knelt and bowed their heads to the ground praying. "This is repeated six times a day in this country of twenty million." Aliyah said as they exited the mosque and hailed a taxi.

"You must be starving", noted Aliyah telling the driver to go to the Damascus Sheraton. "They have good Western food there."

"No! I want to eat as much of the local food as possible, I have the rest of my life for hamburgers" laughed Leda.

They entered the dining room filled with dark-suited businessmen intently discussing projected deals. Lunch consisted of mezzeh, a combination of many small dishes and savories. Leda gasped in surprise at the almost thirty tiny courses that arrived – humus, pureed eggplant with lemon, meat rissoles, stuffed vine leaves, garlic and oil, crushed wheat, parsley, tomato and onion, kebabs of lamb and chicken, pita bread.

After lunch, they went to the Azem Palace, now a Museum, built in alternating layers of black and white stone.

By late afternoon the heat was intense and Aliyah noticed Leda was walking slower.

"Ali, drive us around the city," Leda was appalled by some of the poverty, especially when they came into sections of Palestinian refugees' shacks with children running shoeless and playing in the dirt. As they passed a dilapidated building, Aliyah indicated "This is the Jaramana clinic but you will inspect it later."

Why did poverty abroad inspire more sorrow than the poverty at home? When I travel I am sensitive to beggars and never pass one without giving alms; whereas in New York I look upon street people with derision. In the land of plenty beggars are to blame for their own misfortune, whereas in an unfamiliar land these same people seem to be victims of grave injustice.

"Most of the poverty exists because Syria took in almost 4 million of the poorest Palestinian and Iraqi refugees. Other countries had minimum financial requirements for immigration whereas Syria did not and wound up with the poorest. It also does not get any American funding given to Egypt, Israel and Jordan." Aliyah explained. Leda knew that Syria was a Socialist country but had not realized it had so much charity for refugees.

"I see Mr. Assad's picture everywhere. Is he that popular?"

"The country is ruled by his iron hand. Assad 'won' the last election by a complete majority and is a complete dictator." Leda and Aliyah discussed the political situation late into the night.

The next day at breakfast Leda announced, "Aliyah, today I will go off on my own to do some exploring. But it is my last day of tourism. I am anxious to get to work."

" Be a tourist for a little while longer—once you start working it will be difficult for you to see the beauty of Damascus. I would rather you did not go alone but if you insist please dress very conservatively covering your arms and your legs. Here is a map of Damascus in English and here is a cell phone." Aliyah said in an annoyed tone.

"I am not a child. Do not worry. I want to see for myself what is going on in this city that I have dreamed of visiting all my life" Leda emphatically stated as she put the map in her purse.

The day was sunny and warm and Leda felt overdressed in the long skirt and hat. Aliyah was to meet her at the designated spot when she called on her cell phone. Leda started to go in the direction of Straight Street admiring the unique architecture when she heard the sound of the muezzin. The minarets with the emanating sounds were like needles against the brilliant blue sky. Little passageways and courtyards appeared through open doors. Homes in the old town had the typical Arabic architecture of a relatively plain outside with the marvel of a beautiful, secluded courtyard at the center. This idea was duplicated in the shrouded women, waiting for their beauty to be discovered. *The whole culture has hidden beauty and a mystery. The obvious suddenly is so very primitive when I consider the ostentatious architecture and the nakedness of the women of the West.*

Straight street, the very street Alexander the Great and Pompey marched, and she saw in her mind's eye the armies of the Umayyad Dynasty and the Turks. She imagined the Crusaders in their armor on horseback entering this city. This is where Paul was converted and Lawrence of Arabia met with his faithful Arabs and the pashas of the Ottoman Empire congregated. *The whole panorama of history is here before my eyes.*

Merchants besieged her with embroidered fabrics, brass rings, and amber necklaces. She shuddered in the food section to see sides of cows covered with flies. A young boy with chocolate eyes sold her flowers, beautiful and inexpensive. She could not resist the beauty of some of the people. *Why is this so appealing to me? Was my life so bland and sterile that only this environment brings me to life?"*

She inspected a merchant's damascene metal works, which, Aliyah had warned her, was for tourists and made in China. Leda smiled and shook her head, whereupon he asked her to have some coffee. To Arabs hospitality was a part of their culture. She stopped in his souk and was handed a small cup of steaming, thick, sweet coffee. "Rich American, No?" he said as she noticed that he had no teeth." I - seven children and life hard, hard - bombs, Israeli war, no money food for children." She paid for a poorly made sword noticing some of the false precious stones had already dislodged as he bowed and called for Allah's blessings upon her.

Many stalls with various spices and the aromas were stimulating, giving her an appetite. She saw a restaurant but the menu was in Arabic script so she was puzzled. Leda finally saw some fruit and a teapot and showed the owner by pointing. Leaving a generous tip she left the restaurant into the sweltering heat.

After further wandering Leda realized she was lost. She walked up to a group of women, but they bowed their heads and moved away. She saw some men standing on a corner smoking and approached them, pointing to a street on her map. They all started to gesticulate and point in various directions. A savior appeared in the form of a well-dressed Arab who spoke to her in perfect English and offered to guide her to her destination. She was quite surprised when, at the end of the walk with this distinguished gentleman, he held out his hand. He said "Baksheesh." *Everyone must make a living in their own way.* She reached into her purse for a tip and her cell phone.

CHAPTER 7

That evening, Aliyah had a formal reception to introduce Leda to her friends. A glittering group of people in exotic dress appeared. Silks shot through with gold threads clad some women in saris, a woman in a Chanel suit circulated, and a few heavily veiled women sat silently on the fringes. A man introduced as a Saudi prince, dressed in the purest of white robes with the red and white checked kaffiyah held down by a black band, left Leda breathless. "He is only one of about three thousand princes." said Aliyah, throwing some cold water on her excitement. Leda felt she was at the center of a mysterious and exotic world. Fruit juices were passed around, as was champagne for the western contingent.

The names of so many people all at once left Leda in a quandary. At last Aliyah said, "And this is our great good friend from the British Embassy, Lord Denver." Leda turned to see a balding, thin man who appeared to be smaller than he actually was due to a shrinking, inward quality.

His face was thin and colorless with blond eyebrows and almost translucent eyes. He apologized profusely for not having come to meet Leda earlier but he had some matters at the Embassy to finish. "Of course there are no matters as important as being at the beck and call of my beautiful hostess, Aliyah." Leda observed the look of longing in Lord Denver's pale, watery eyes as he turned his gaze on Aliyah. Aliyah turned and left them alone.

"Lord Denver, how long have you been with the Embassy?"

"My dear, far too long. It is a difficult tour of duty since as you know the British stand in just a little better stead in the populace than the Americans, who are despised." he confided.

"But I spent today alone in Damascus and I found no hostility from the people. Perhaps the enmity towards Americans is not at all what you perceive. Your opinion could be the result of a few unfortunate incidents."

"Syria needs tourists and the merchants will be friendly to obtain your money, but you should never forget that at this crucial time in history there is much resentment of the current political stance of the United States," he said apologetically. As he continued his eyes shifted to Aliyah greeting a new guest and he gestured toward her, "Now there is one woman who is in danger. She refuses to divest herself of her American interests and friends and is very vocal about greater understanding. There are many people in Damascus that consider her an enemy of Islam."

"Enemy! You can't be serious."

"I wish I were joking. She is a great friend of mine, perhaps my only true friend here. After all, let me ask you a question. What is the source of all evil?"

Leda thought this was a joke, but then saw the serious expression on Lord Denver's face. "Why, money, it must be money!"

"No, my dear, it is the British. It was the British who carved up the Middle East and caused all our modern troubles."

No wonder Lord Denver considered the British to be the source of all evil. Theft and betrayal and injustice were the recipe for a century of hatred resulting from the actions of the British.

Lord Denver, unaware of Leda's familiarity with the situation continued, "It was the British that gave a part of Palestine for a Jewish homeland after considering other places in Africa and America. But the Jews insisted on their historical homeland and started to settle there and buy additional land from the Palestinians."

Leda seemed to absorb every word with breathless interest because she was curious about the official British position. Lord Denver, flattered by the attention, took another glass of champagne and continued, "Then the Jewish people started their insistent campaign for the State of Israel as a reaction to the millions of Jews killed in World War II so Israel was born in 1948."

All of this would be a great story if it did not ignore the 750,000 Palestinians driven from their homes in order to make this possible in 1948. Independence Day for the Israelis was the Day of Disaster for the Palestinians.

Aliyah had quietly joined them and Lord Denver turned to her with a bow and a shy smile. Aliyah interjected, "The 750,000 refugees of 1948 have grown to 4 million because of the war of 1967 and further hostilities. They are now spread out over the Occupied West Bank, Gaza, Jordan, Syria and Lebanon. The United Nations in numerous resolutions holds up the principles of international justice by the right of return of the Palestinian people but the United States is always unequivocally on the side of Israel." Aliyah's voice contained barely suppressed rage.

With his increased audience, Lord Denver preened a little and with renewed vigor continued, "In 1948 Israel claimed fifty-four percent of Palestine for its state. After the war of 1967 the Palestinians were confined to twenty-two of the land and now because of the settlements Palestinians control only nine percent of their original territory."

Lord Denver paused for emphasis and added, "In all the talks of a two state solution all that the Palestinians want is twenty-two percent of the land. Even that is now impossible due to the facts on the ground – huge settlement cities on Palestinian land heavily colonized and subsidized by the government whose end game is all of Palestine." Lord Denver reeled off all these facts without emotion as if he frequently had to give this history lesson to tourists. *No wonder it is called diplomacy - it is a way to avoid judgment or right and wrong. Diplomats exist to gloss over facts.*

"What can be done, when there is no hope?" Leda asked.

Lord Denver shrugged his narrow shoulders; "The winners will write the history and the identity of the winners is obvious."

He then kissed Aliyah's hand and took his leave.

Leda turned to the waiter and asked for some scotch as she saw Talib observing her from across the room. She noticed her strong reaction to him and for a brief moment was disturbed that she had not worn her form-fitting, purple silk dress. *This is ridiculous, it would make no difference if I wore a gunnysack, my God, he is young enough to be my son.*

She found herself standing next to a Jewish Rabbi. "I see you are drinking scotch so you must be an American.

"Why yes" Leda replied smiling, my name is Leda Eimont from Connecticut."

"My name is Leon Lerner. You are not too far from my home in Westchester. I have a dual citizenship with Israel so I go back and forth. I come to Damascus to take care of my Jewish congregation."

"Jewish population in Damascus?"

"Yes. Damascus has a Jewish population and the government allows me to come to provide spiritual guidance."

"And you have dual citizenship?"

"About half of Israelis have dual citizenship, mostly with the United States and Britain."

"Would that not be a problem if the countries went to war with one another? I do know American boys go to Israel to fulfill their military service."

The Rabbi laughed. "Impossible that would never happen. And in the hypothetical event of war Israel would need help more."

There is no man that can serve two masters and Israel was more important.

The talk segued into politics and the current situation of the United States and Islam. He explained the hostilities in terms of a political and economic basis rather than a religious basis. During her discussion with the Rabbi she again sensed eucalyptus and felt a strong physical presence. She turned to see Talib standing by her side.

"Rabbi, you are one of the few that do not feel the power of hatred between us." Talib said joining the conversation. "Through the centuries there has been so much blood flowing and so many resentments boiling that it is beyond discussion. Israel is ruling the world these days through its manipulation of the United States. Israel is in the process of extermination of the whole Palestinian peoples and taking over all the territory. Is this justice? Do you not go to the Palestinian camps and see the results of Jewish 'justice'? Do you not see that the West Bank is a prison and Gaza is a concentration camp?"

The Rabbi looked at Talib and said quietly, "You will never understand that small country trying to defend itself in a sea of hostility. Why the suicide bombers? Do you think that will bring about peace?"

Talib looked at the Rabbi, turned abruptly, and walked out into the verandah while the Rabbi said good-bye to Leda, wished her a pleasant stay, and took his leave. She saw Aliyah run to the verandah and have a very animated discussion with Talib. Leda decided not to interfere.

All she had known on a theoretical, historical basis was being played out in reality. The turmoil of this region of the world reflected her emotional involvement. Leda always felt sorry for the underdog, and the most pathetic international underdog in the world was Palestine.

What can I do to help? No one in power back home seemed to care. She saw Talib come back from the verandah with an expression of disgust. As he saw Leda he broke into a smile. *Is Talib truly concerned with the fate of the Palestinians? Perhaps he will let me know how to be of use to his and Aliyah's cause.*

As he approached her she warmly returned his smile. *Or does my interest in Talib spring from a more basic feeling than altruism?*

CHAPTER 8

"Leda, are you ready to work?" Aliyah called out on a sunny morning three days after her arrival. "Your cartons of supplies have arrived." They prepared for the trip to the Khan Eshieh refugee camp to unpack the cartons and introduce Leda to the clinic. Aliyah said that Talib would help them with the initial arrangements.

"You realize that all the latest advances in medicine and infection control are not available to us. In the United States you have disposable gloves for all procedures, but here, we are lucky to have a pair for operations and even then we wash them with soap and water for reuse. There is a dearth of needles and disposable ones are beyond our means. Heaven knows how many people we infect. Anesthetic is hard to come by so you must get hardened against the screaming. I hope you are really up to this work. You come from such a different world." Aliyah said apologetically as they got into the car.

"Of course I understand the limitations but I am a physician, not a debutante. I have come to help."

"At times I have lost the zeal to do as much as I could because it seems so hopeless -the throngs of the ill, the scarcity of supplies. Sometimes I just want to go home and forget about it all. I want to leave this bottomless pit of suffering because it seems that there is never any progress."

Leda braced herself against this tirade with determination. "To do something always trumps doing nothing. We are just expected to do the best we can, which we will do." *What horror will be absorbed in my brain? I want to avoid unforgettable images of suffering but it seems that I will not escape the brutality of this life. Arthur warned me about this.*

Aliyah's driver headed towards the mountains and away from the desert. The roads were surprisingly smooth and Aliyah's lecture droned on to the sounds of the motor. "There are about 350,000 Palestinian refugees here displaced by Israel - 250,000 made their way into Syrian society but about 90,000 are in 10 camps located throughout the country. We are going to Khan Eshieh, the largest one with 13,000 refugees, and only one clinic staffed by volunteer doctors." Leaving the city, Leda noticed more and more women who were veiled and dressed in black, in contrast to the more modern looking women in Damascus.

They arrived at the clinic, a wooden barn, mid-morning in the blazing sun. A line of people, some women holding small children, others sitting grimacing in pain were waiting. Inside, six men in wrinkled, bloodstained jackets moved about a row of beds and chairs. Leda almost did not recognize Talib in full Arab garb. He was cutting apart some of the cartons with their soon-to-be-expired drugs that Leda obtained from drug company representatives convincing them of the desperate need in refugee camps. She also beseeched her colleagues for all their old medical instruments. As she observed the two huge containers with pride and satisfaction Talib looked up and said, "Leda, you are remarkable for all your efforts. I wouldn't have thought that an American princess could accomplish so much for what is certainly an unpopular cause in America."

To set up a semblance of a clinic was a challenge. Leda looked around and saw water tanks placed near the ceiling fed the few sinks in the area. The stoves heated boiling water for instrument sterilization. Leda could not imagine what kind of help she could provide in circumstances so foreign from her training in health care. She started scrubbing down all surfaces with soap and water and disinfectant and placing some instruments at each station - blood pressure cuffs, thermometers, and bandages.

"We must start seeing patients. Some of these people have been here since yesterday," said Aliyah as she led Leda to a station. "This is Ali; he will help you with translation and also assist you for the more painful procedures. Leda put on her gloves, buttoned her white coat and took a deep breath.

The first patient was a semi-comatose old man with a huge swelling in his jaw. His eyes were glazed and he was feverish. He could not speak, but his daughter told Ali that the swelling started following a bout of terrific pain in his jaw and he had not been able to eat for a week. Leda saw that he was dehydrated and started an IV. She looked in his mouth with some difficulty and could see that it was a huge dental abscess. They had no x-ray equipment and dentistry was as foreign to her as neurosurgery since she spent most of her life in ophthalmology. She ran to get Talib and explained the situation to him. He came over and disconnected the IV. "We use these only on young people in serious situations, not for an old man with a toothache! Just take the tooth out!"

Leda started to look for a syringe with anesthetic when Talib spoke in Arabic to Ali who produced some pliers. "How will I know which tooth to extract?"

Talib looked at Leda with incomprehension. "Just take out all of them near the swollen site! And you must hurry! There are many critically ill people here!" She jabbed the area with a cartridge of anesthetic as she tried to recall the three lectures she had in medical school about dentistry.

"No! No! We do not need anesthetic for this. All the pus in the area will dilute it, so it won't be effective anyway. We need the anesthetic for more important things!" Talib shouted to her looking over his shoulder while trying to set a fractured leg.

Leda grabbed the pliers and said a silent prayer as perspiration poured down her arms and forehead. She could not remember being so tense and under such pressure since medical school when a hostile professor had grilled her for an hour in front of the class. Even now, she shuddered with the memory. She inserted the pliers and with Ali forcing the mouth open she applied pressure to the most likely culprit and recalled, "rotate and pull, rotate and pull." With the man screaming and her hand shaking, she finally gave her whole strength into the final effort and heard a loud crack. The bloody stump emerged followed by a cupful of pus.

She saw Talib standing in back of her smiling, "This is medicine Arab style."

She barely had time to wash when a small boy was brought to her with an enormous eye infection. She had only read about Trachoma in medical texts, but she had never actually seen a case. Prevalent in hot, dry, Mediterranean countries, this contagious disease was spread by flies. She knew that without treatment, it would lead to blindness. The infection healed by scar tissue that eventually clouded the entire cornea. Treatment was with antibiotics and Leda sighed with relief and satisfaction that her tetracycline ophthalmic ointment would produce relief and a subsequent cure.

Today, I prevented blindness, set fractures, sutured wounds and diagnosed cancers: something concrete and real. In my practice I was so proud of my decorated office with fresh flowers, classical music, original oil paintings, a receptionist with a British accent, and nurses dressed in sparkling white. My patients, not to be kept waiting even a few minutes, demanded tranquilizers, pain killers, and sedation to stave off even the slightest discomfort. Lasix surgeries and cataracts filled my days and blended into boredom. After cataract removal patients could see their aged faces much more clearly and wanted recommendations for plastic surgery. Cosmetic surgeons started to send me cases of champagne with notes, "Keep up with those cataracts!" I can't reconcile this clinic and my private practice under the same heading of medicine.

Exhausted after her first day of work, Leda returned home with Aliyah and went straight to her room for a bath. Coming out of the water, drying herself, she observed her body in the mirrored wall. Her small, round breasts, her figure sculpted by regular exercise classes, her long shapely legs pleased her. But *what was all this hidden pulchritude for, all this effort to maintain a myth of ageless sexuality*? Now, with her long flowing robes and scarves, she seemed completely invisible. The sadness was especially palpable when she thought of Talib. "I must be insane to have these thoughts," she said aloud to herself as she lay down on the bed.

Leda rose in the darkness, disoriented as to time and place, and fumbled for her eyeglasses, found them perched on top of her head, and saw that it was midnight. She opened the door to find a tray covered with Damask. She took the tray into her room uncovering the cloth saw a lamb and cucumber sandwich, a pot of tea, and a note:

I did not want to interrupt your dreams – hope this holds you until morning – a big English breakfast planned. I could understand your exhaustion. Aliyah.

When she finished her meal, Leda opened her door to return the tray to the hall table. Still ravenous she remembered the big bowl of ripe fruit always present in the downstairs hallway. As she started down the stairs, she saw a faint light and heard a murmuring of conversation. Not being dressed, she crouched on the landing and saw five men standing by the front door. The only one she recognized was Talib who was in Arab garb as was one other man, the rest were in dark suits and one, very distinguished looking, had salt and pepper hair. All of them left and Talib closed the door. As he walked to the back of the house, Leda made a swift retreat back into her room. *Where were Aliyah and the servants? Why didn't Talib leave with the rest?* She quickly turned around and went back to bed.

She could not fall asleep that night tortured with horrific thoughts of the clinic, the mystery of Talib and her strong reaction to him. *Perhaps the decision to come here was a mistake. Arthur was right. Home is a safe and known haven. I do not need this trauma, this difficulty, this soul-searching at my age after a life spent in quiet luxury and contemplation.* She tossed and turned and finally decided that if she had a piece of fruit she could fall asleep. She tossed on a white silk robe and gently pried open her door. All was dark in the hallway to the stairwell but further there was a faint light. No one was in sight this time so she worked her way down to the front hall.

As she pulled out one orange and a bunch of grapes, she saw Talib approach from the living room. Their eyes locked in mutual surprise. Leda held up the fruit with a smile by way of explanation but Talib did not smile. He continued to walk straight at her until he stood in front of her so close that she felt his body press against her. In her whole life she had never had a greater sensation of nakedness. The thin robe dissolved, Talib's cotton robe dissolved and she knew that without a touch they were exposed to one another. She had a sensation of not only his body, but also hers, in all vulnerability. She looked up at him, no longer smiling. "What are you doing here? Where is Aliyah?"

Talib did not reply. She felt his warm breath on her forehead. At last, after an eternity of Leda's heart racing, he whispered, "I am intruding on your personal space. I am sorry, it makes Westerners very uncomfortable." He abruptly turned and went out through the front door, gently closing it behind him. Nothing had happened, not a touch, not a gesture, but Leda knew what had happened as surely as if it had occurred by force in a dark alley in New York. She felt ravished, consumed. *Am I this vulnerable to this unknown Arab that mere closeness would lead me to believe I was violated?*

The morning found her tired and confused. Breakfast was splendid with scrambled eggs, kippers, bangers, jams, toast and cake. Aliyah was aware of a change in Leda that she attributed to finally being exposed to the reality of her commitment. Leda, reviewing her last twenty-four hours, slowly went upstairs to her room to prepare for another trip to the refugee camp. She was looking at the little picture of Arthur with Frodo that she always kept near when she heard Aliyah call to her, "Leda, telephone from the States!"

Leda was glad. It must be Arthur – a clear and familiar, loving voice coming to her from home. She wanted to be rid of this terrible ambivalence; never before did she have any doubts about her life or her choices. She wanted the safety of home without the bother of this painful reexamination of her inner needs. She went downstairs with a smile and picked up the phone. "Arthur!" she said with the anticipation of one saved.

"Sorry, this is Dr. Kaminsky over at Columbia Presbyterian. Mrs. Lodge, I am sorry to inform you that we have a serious condition on our hands. Your husband was hospitalized here last night and he insisted that we do not call you, but the situation is grave and I think it would warrant coming home."

"I am a physician myself. Could you tell me the nature of the problem?" Leda found herself asking the question with a degree of professionalism astounding even to her, as if she were inquiring about a stranger's condition.

"Your husband has advanced cancer and the operation is scheduled for this afternoon. In his condition it will be a high risk surgery."

"Can't you put it off until I get there, I should be able to manage in twenty-four hours?"

"I'm sorry but the timing is critical."

"I am coming," was all that Leda could say as she replaced the receiver and realized it was wet due to the perspiration from her icy hands. She was in a state of complete shock.

Advanced cancer? This could not be true. There were no signs, no symptoms. Of course Arthur did not have the energy of his youth but that was to be expected in a man of his age. What had I missed? And now to be here on the other side of the world caring for strangers when the love of my life needed me the most.

CHAPTER 9

Leda packed a small carry-on bag as Aliyah reassured her that all would go well. Leda, silent and guilty, could not help but make a connection between Arthur's current state and her feelings for Talib. "Leda, the car is waiting!" cried Aliyah. The driver rushed them to the airport where Air France, with first class completely booked, gave Leda a business class seat. She observed a brutal security check. Everyone was searched, patted down, and security cut into some suitcases with knives. Leda looked at the scene with horror, but Aliyah assured her it was for her own safety since flights coming from Damascus were highly suspect. Close to flight time Aliyah made a phone call and managed to get a small man in a business suit to come and get Leda priority through security.

During the flight, she did the only thing she could—she took her blue sleeping pill and slept. Paris was just a blur of changing planes at De Gaulle since she had a chance of making an earlier connection. She ran to a Continental flight just before the doors closed. In her coach seat, the only one available, she could not sleep and the bright lights all the way home left her in an anxious state. *If I had my computer or my medical texts I would read the latest about cancer and the new miracle drugs. I know that information would ward off terror. If the clinical facts are known, the situation becomes manageable.*

Arrival at JFK was a nightmare because of the many incoming flights. She saw that every Middle-Eastern looking man who was under 50 was pulled aside. The man in front of her was also pulled aside but not before she heard him saying, "But I am Jewish."

Why the racial profiling? Both Arabs and Jews were Semites racially. With such variety in humans, how could one be judged on the basis of another? But this was government policy often dissociated from the welfare of the people. There was a ruling clique, and their perception of power and how to hold on to it was paramount. The United States government was run at the behest of the people who contributed the most money and owned the media. An aura of democracy and governing according to the will of the people was conferred by the polls.

Leda hailed a cab to the hospital; it seemed as if nineteen-hour trip had taken an eternity. Rush hour made the trip through Manhattan excruciating long until finally, she was at the entrance. Giving the cabby a hundred-dollar bill, murmuring, "keep the change," she sprinted inside. The dreadlocked young man behind the information desk could not find Lodge on the register. Leda paged Dr. Kaminsky who immediately answered and said to wait in the lobby. A short, fat, baldheaded man with a noticeable limp approached her off the elevator. The minute she saw his face she knew the news was not good. "Mrs. Lodge, or Dr. Eimont I should say, come with me." She followed him in a trance up the elevator, through the automated door marked Critical Care to a small room with sofas and a television in the corner.

"We did everything we could, but, your husband had a stroke during the immediate post-op period and for the last six hours he has been brain-dead. Of course he is on machines. Would you like to see him?" Leda was so tired and in shock that she could not speak. "There is no rush. I understand that you just came back from Damascus. I am sorry to say that the situation looks hopeless. We had already discussed disconnecting the machines but I said you were on your way."

Leda looked over to the muted television. The quiz contestants were smiling and one man was jumping up and down. *Did not the whole world end with this news? Could so many things continue in the face of my world stopping?* She looked down at her hand with its prominent veins and brown spots. Were these hands still alive? She imagined them caressing Arthur's hands that always held her world—safe, secure, known. The physician in Leda took over as she faced Dr. Kaminsky. "Doctor, what happened? He was getting more tired but that is common at his age. What was the diagnosis?"

"I diagnosed mesothelioma and have been treating Arthur with experimental drugs for six months. He wanted no one to know until he told you himself. He said a trip to Montana by himself would be a time to think things through. Did he not discuss this with you? I was astonished that you were in Syria in spite of Arthur's terminal illness."

"Mesothelioma! Leda gasped. "It cannot be, Arthur was an executive all his life and you are talking about a cancer caused by asbestos. This is common in laborers, in factory workers. No, you must have made a huge mistake! He has never even been near asbestos."

Dr. Kaminsky opened the chart and read, "Navy service on the USS Union, patient remembers being told to go clear the ammunition room of asbestos shelf covers. For two weeks Navy issue masks worn, experienced rash the following month, no symptoms until six months ago when patient experienced shortness of breath."

"My God! That was when he left high school at seventeen." said a shocked Leda. *It had been dormant for fifty years and returned to kill him by the wild growth of the mucous cells in the chest wall lining. As these rogue cells proliferated they produced quarts of thick mucus which filled the space into which the lungs could expand. A slow suffocation! My Arthur! And I did not know!*

Dr. Kaminsky put his arm on Leda's shoulder, "Please, it must be a shock to you. The cancer could have been contained for a few months more, but due to the severe pain, we needed to do emergency surgery. The procedure in itself went well, but due to his compromised state, he had a stroke. It could also be associated with the experimental medicine he was on." The doctor's beeper went off, "Please excuse me, I have to go. We will speak later after you see your husband."

Leda jumped up and went out to the nurses' station and identified herself. "I want to see Arthur Lodge immediately."

A petite Asian nurse said, "Right this way, Mrs. Lodge," and added, "I am so sorry." They passed double doors into a large room with multiple beds and all the paraphernalia of modern death. Surrounded by curtains and four IV units and hooked up to a breathing machine and a heart monitor, lay Arthur.

"Darling, my dearest darling, take me with you to where you are. Wherever it is, I would rather be there than here without you," she whispered as her tears wet the white sheet over his chest covering a long incision. She felt his cold hand. "Please nurse, a blanket, he is freezing!"

The ICU nurse brought some white cotton blankets and she put them around Arthur. She also brought a recliner by the bedside, "Mrs. Lodge, please sit down, you look very white." Leda started to feel a warmth and darkness in the base of her skull. As she sat down, she was handed a glass of orange juice.

She held Arthur's hand for hours telling him all that he was her father, brother, son, lover and best friend. *Of course, Arthur did not want to tell me of his illness, and did not stop my Syrian trip. He wanted to protect me. Any book he gave me would have all the pages that would cause me sadness already torn out. Arthur called me "my little one." With Arthur to return to, I was free to take risks, explore, and achieve, since if I failed, I always had my safety net.*

She remembered their first meeting at a tennis camp in Amherst in September. Arthur was there to play with professionals and she was hoping to improve her game as a challenge to Leslie. He was well travelled, older, sophisticated, handsome and divorced. Leda was impressed but hastened to inform him that she was already engaged. Arthur said he understood her constraints but would like to spend some time with her in Manhattan anyway. They had dinners, took long walks in Central Park, drove to Vermont to see the leaves turn and talked with the acute excitement of peering into someone else's soul. By November there was no longer any doubt, she belonged to this man.

The doctor returned. "Dr. Eimont, there is really nothing more to be done. Your husband is brain dead and you must rest before you must face disconnecting the machines." Leda looked at the doctor with a fixed stare and did not answer.

How could I possibly give up? There must be more that I could do. After all, I am a physician with important connections. Yes. That's it. Don't sit there like a dummy, a stupid uneducated woman, taking their word for it. Fight. Show that you know medicine. That no one can push you around. Arthur's life is at stake! Having reached this degree of anger, Leda felt a surge of energy, of hope, of action. She stood up and had to sit down. She had never felt so weak. She looked at her Bulgari watch, her last birthday present from Arthur, the diamonds encircled the gold dials pointing to 6:15. She motioned to a passing nurse and asked for coffee.

"Why yes, Mrs. Lodge, I let you rest in that recliner but you need more than coffee." She returned in a few minutes with a full tray but Leda only drank the coffee. The crisp nurse let Leda become aware of her own state of grooming. More important things were at stake. She pulled an address book out of her Hermes bag and saw her friend Sophia's number.

Sophia was always extreme – in looks and in personality. She had dark, flashing eyes and masses of curly hair. She had confided that because of her Greek background and hair in grammar school she was called Medusa to her tearful horror. She tried everything to hide her hair – greasy creams, irons and scarves with no success in improving her looks until college when she emerged in the height of fashion with long skirts, embroidered blouses, and sandals which complemented her untamed mane.

At Sophia's wedding to Dr. Conrad Milo, Leda was shocked at her choice of this colorless, humorless, emaciated man. Sophia spent every waking hour trying to please Conrad. Her extravagant cooking habits were subsumed with his vegetarian preference; their home designed with little input from her. Her two sons, as they matured and developed their own personalities, had all the genes of their father and none from their mother. She now lived on the outskirts of Boston in a glass cube surrounded by emotional icicles. To get out of the cold she continued to sacrifice her time and energy for anyone that she perceived she could help. She called Boston and a sleepy Sophia answered.

"Leda, where are you? Still in Damascus?"

"Sophia, please get Conrad on the line, this is an emergency. I am in New York and Arthur is dying." Leda felt that by doing something, anything, she was in control again.

"Oh no!" And then, "Conrad!"

"Conrad is coming, he was just leaving for the hospital. Here he is."

"Conrad Milos here." His official voice reassured Leda. *Yes, help was on its way.*

"Conrad, this is Leda. I am calling from Columbia-Presbyterian in New York. Arthur had a stroke during a surgical procedure for mesothelioma and now he is in a coma. Who is the best person in New York?"

"I'm so sorry. In cases of coma the best person is Irving

Horowitz. He has consulted on some of my cases. He could do an evaluation. Is there anything I could do?"

"Apparently it was an emergency and they operated right away. At least it was in a good institution but the doctor, a Dr. Kaminsky. Have you heard of him?"

No," said Conrad hesitantly, "but he could be a good guy and the institution is a good one. I am sure all was done. Sophia is standing here. She wants to say something."

"I will be there on the next flight Leda. You can't be alone." Sophia said with a voice filled with compassion and determination. Leda did not have the energy to argue with her.

Leda placed a call to Dr. Horowitz and said that she was a friend of Dr. Conrad Milos. In a few minutes a gruff voice said "Horowitz." Leda explained the situation and said she wanted another evaluation. Dr. Horowitz said he would come to the hospital the following day as a special favor for Conrad who had done heart surgery on his mother. "Good fellow, that Conrad." Putting down the phone, Leda sighed with relief as she saw a spark of hope.

Returning to the bedside, she found Dr. Kaminsky and a group of residents surrounding Arthur. Seeing her, he introduced Leda as Dr. Leda Eimont and questioned the residents about the ophthalmological signs of coma, presumably for her benefit. Leda was thoroughly embarrassed to consider that she did not do the examination herself. After all, this was her field and the one thing she herself could have done, she did not do. She grabbed an ophthalmoscope from a resident and opened one of Arthur's lids. An ophthalmic ointment to prevent abrasions covered the eye. She hardly recognized those bright blue eyes that she loved. His chest rose and fell; she could hear his heart beat. She switched on the light of the ophthalmoscope. The pupil was fixed. *He was dead—a living dead man.*

Sophie arrived that evening and took Leda in her arms and said, "Leda, no matter what, you are going to the company apartment for a rest." Arthur used the apartment for nights he had late meetings. "You must go and get some sleep. Nothing will happen in the next twelve hours and you look completely haggard. You will need all your strength in the next few days." Sophia took their bags and hailed a cab. She walked into the apartment, went into one of the bedrooms, and realized that Arthur would never be there with her again.

The zipper of her skirt pinching her waist woke her and Leda realized with a start that it was morning and she was in the New York apartment. The bedroom had an aura of strangeness, hostility, a cold dryness in the air. She stood up with a sharp realization of a full bladder from the gallons of coffee she had imbibed, and almost staggered to the bathroom. There the mirrored walls sent a message of an old, disheveled, wrinkled woman. She drank some water, undressed, and ran a bath while scrubbing her teeth.

Sophia had hot coffee and breakfast ready. She found herself enormously hungry and ate all her scrambled eggs. Walking to the refrigerator for some milk she glanced up and saw an old note in Arthur's handwriting. *SEND FLOWERS TO LEDA.* He was always writing himself notes. She felt a spasm in her chest. As she sat down at the kitchen table, Sophia placed the mail by her side. A stack of advertisements and a letter addressed to her in Damascus and marked

"RETURNED INSUFFICIENT POSTAGE." It was a handwritten letter from Arthur. She tore it open:

My Darling Leda,

I do not know how to begin. Some time ago I was feeling unusually tired and went to see my doctor. After a series of tests he said that I had a very serious lung condition at a relatively late stage. I underwent some experimental treatment but was told it was not working. I had to come to grips with this news on my own and that is why I went to Montana. I did not want suffocating concern and hysterical sorrow to ruin our last few weeks together. I did not want to burden you with the ugliness of my illness. When you decided to go to the Middle East, I was concerned for your safety but in a way relieved that I could spare you so much anguish. How I wish I could have been diagnosed with a heart condition or an operable cancer – I do want to live and be with you. Now that my disease is advancing I am no longer so brave and long to have you near me. I am sorry for what I will have to put you through but I need you. I could have called you but did not know how to say the words.

All my love, Arthur

CHAPTER 10

A cloudy day in Manhattan was the setting for a thousand thoughts paralyzing her movements. Leda was a fly caught in amber. *If Arthur were dead, there would be no more considerations, only mourning. Due to the advancements of modern medicine, I will have to make the decision to end his life. It is only a formality, a signature, a release, but there are repercussions. No matter how little life was left, I will know forever that I destroyed it, erased all hope. As long as there is life it trumps death. I especially value Arthur's life and my religion teaches that only God may take a life. But I know that a quick and painless death is among the greatest gifts of life.*

She remembered her dog Max. The dog was the recipient of all the love and nurturing that she never expended on a child. When Max reached fourteen, he showed all the signs of senility and the veterinarian told Leda that it was time to put him down. She nursed Max at home for a few weeks but could not bring herself to end his life. One day she came home and the dog bed was empty. Arthur had done it for her so that all she had to do was mourn because he had taken the painful decision from her. She needed Arthur now again to take the decision to end his life from her.

How could she make such a decision on her own? She called her attorney and asked them to fax Arthur's medical directives to the apartment. She looked over the document where he had checked "artificial means to prolong life" NO.

She reminisced about the autumn day they had gone to the attorney to draw up their wills after a wonderful two-martini lunch. The leaves were a colorful panorama of colors. They were giddy with laughter while they were waiting in the hushed and plush reception room of Hardy, Peebles, Peebles and Worth. "You will be a rich woman with this will. Enough reason for murder," Arthur winked at her.

Leda, in a red suit, pushed back her blonde hair, "And what good would that do me in prison. After all, it is always the spouse."

"You would be clever enough to come up with the ultimate murder. No one would suspect."

"Yes," Leda said with a smile. You would die after eating yew berry pie."

"Brilliant!" said Arthur laughing.

The lawyer, himself emaciated and sickly-looking, pulled out the advance directives after they had signed their wills. "You will certainly want the peace of mind knowing that your wishes are followed should anything untoward happen."

Arthur laughed as he signed *do not resuscitate*. "This is preferable to be nursed by Leda."

Was this joking afternoon contained in this final document? Was it truly meant to be a matter of life and death? The alternatives- a lifetime in a coma—not really alive, being turned every two hours to prevent bed sores, artificial breathing, artificial intake of food, catheters to take away the urine, and enemas every day to remove the fecal matter. In a bad facility, patients would normally die of an infection within the first six months, but in a good facility? Life could be extended for years. Is this what I would want for myself? Is this what Arthur would want? But once the decision is made, it is irrevocable. He would be dead and I would be responsible. Could I live with that? Even with a signed document, it is me who is responsible in the end.

She dressed in a black suit as befitted her mood and left the apartment with Sophia. In the elevator she looked at her cell phone turned off during her flight and saw that she had thirty calls. Scrolling down she saw many familiar names but her heart stopped when she saw voicemail from Dr. Talib al-Zawahiri. "Leda, I am so sorry. You know I cannot be with you but you are in my thoughts."

Entering Arthur's room she saw sorrow in abundance. *Is this the punishment for my lovely life? - The vengeance of a cruel and spiteful God. No, No! Holy Mary, Mother of God.* She got on her knees, holding Arthur's hand as she reverted to her most basic instinct of prayer. It was in this pose that Dr. Horowitz found Leda. "Dr. Eimont, I studied the chart and I would like to examine the patient. I hate to intrude but my time is very limited this morning." A flustered Leda got up off of her knees and extended her hand. He was a very tall, elegant man in a custom-made charcoal suit. He could have been from the pages of *Gentleman's Quarterly*. Leda watched as he did a full physical examination and studied the thick chart.

"Apparently, the mesothelioma was not diagnosed because

of the atypical symptoms. The diaphragm's nerve fibers were invaded causing the unbearable pain. The operation to sever the nerves was carried out with success but two hours later, a drop in blood pressure revealed break-through bleeding. A second operation was done to find and stop the bleeder. But, as is frequently the case, the heart stopped and was revived but it placed Mr. Lodge in a coma. A subsequent stroke was the final blow. The fixed pupils indicate midbrain damage. There is decerebrate rigidity and no response to stimuli. I'm sorry, Dr. Eimont, but your husband is dead."

"Is there no hope?"

"Dr. Eimont, you are a physician. You can answer that question yourself." And with that Dr. Horowitz was gone, leaving behind him only a whiff of Chanel's *Homme*. As if on cue, Sophia was by her side enveloping her in warmth and said she had called Father Delos to give the Last Sacraments and he would arrive within the hour.

"Leda, my dearest friend" said Father Delos "I can appreciate the torment you are going through but you know the Church does not require any artificial prolonging of life. You, as a Catholic, must above all know that life does not end here on earth. Don't be afraid to let go. It is not your decision to let Arthur die. God made that decision some time ago. You are just letting his body go in peace. His soul is already gone."

Leda trembling signed the paper and clung to Arthur as she realized it was her last moment with him. Leaving the room Leda pronounced, "The Navy killed Arthur. As a seventeen-year-old boy he was assigned to strip the gunnery room of asbestos. There was no follow up on these veterans. He should have been cared for and considered a hero." In her agony, she told Sophia and Father Delos "The government murdered my Arthur."

"Do not say Arthur was murdered by the United States," countered Sophia, "not all bad things in life can be attributed to an evil villain."

"Do not be naïve." Leda said with sarcasm. "You may be patriotic but I know you are intelligent enough to realize that the government is not all flags and apple pie. There are considerations of power, of money. Human life is just an expendable factor to their goal. For the government, as Stalin said, one death is a tragedy, a million dead is just a statistic."

Sophia looked at this argument with increasing discomfort. "The asbestos was still an unknown hazard. Arthur's commanding officers would not have exposed them to such danger knowingly." Sophia could see the hatred in Leda's eyes and wanted to defuse her emotions. She knew this was a reaction, a desire to blame someone for her pain. She was afraid her intense blame would follow Leda for the rest of her life. She would not forgive the government of the United States.

Dr. Kaminsky stopped further discussion as he walked into the reception room and said in a grave voice, "You can go in."

They went back into the room and she saw Arthur, or what was Arthur. His face had changed as if he had lost his substance. It was a face collapsed, almost unrecognizable— the mask of death. He was white and when she kissed him he was cold. Arthur was gone. She had read that the body actually loses a few grams when death occurs—is that the weight of life? She felt pain but also relief. At least it was over.

"The attendants will come to take him to the hospital morgue where his body will await the arrival of your funeral director," said the grey-haired nurse in a rote way. She saw the look on Leda's face and added; "He can't feel anything now, dear. Take your time to say goodbye." The nurse unhooked the machines and pulled the curtain around the bed. Leda stayed bent over the body for what seemed hours held by Sophia's comforting arms.

She took one more look at Arthur and realized they would be putting him in cold storage. She felt how cold he was already and she took the extra blankets and wrapped them around Arthur. She reached up and took one last look at his eyes before closing them. She kissed his hands. She wanted to curl up by his side as she had done in all their years of marriage. She wanted to go with him.

CHAPTER 11

In Connecticut, a plethora of phone messages, family arriving, and friends with inquiries intruded. Within an hour of her return her friend Leslie, a corporate executive, appeared. "My darling Leda, I just heard. What a shock when Sophie called me. I called all our friends and told them that Arthur is in a coma but I did not realize until this minute that he had passed."

"He did not pass, Leslie. Arthur died."

Talks with the funeral director resulted in plans for cremation and a private High Mass. Then, in accordance with Arthur's wishes, there would be a free performance at Carnegie Hall of Verdi's *Requiem*. At their wedding, Leda quoted TS Eliot's poem "the world ends not with a bang but with a whimper" and that she wanted to end her single days not with a whimper but with a bang. At the time, she did not make a connection to the slang for "bang." Arthur always enjoyed telling the story so much that when he first heard the Verdi *Requiem* he was amazed that it was the loudest music he had ever heard. "What a requiem, Leda, Arthur joked, play it at my funeral—I want to go out with a bang".

The funeral was held in St. Mary's Catholic Church. On a wedding anniversary Arthur gave Leda a platinum and diamond necklace and a slip of paper. "Here, this will be an even better present." She opened the note, *"Arthur Lodge has been converted to the Catholic faith."* As Leda looked at him in surprise he said, "Well you did say 'forever' in our vows- and how could we wind up together in a Catholic cemetery if I did not do this?" Arthur's ashes resided in an urn in front of the altar next to a serious official corporate photograph. Leda, tranquilized by her doctor went through the High Mass too numb to even say a prayer.

Leda insisted Sophia and Leslie stay with her as they made arrangements for the concert at Carnegie Hall on a Monday night when there were no other performances. It was impossible to get famous singers at such short notice and the orchestra needed some extra musicians so the best students from Julliard were recruited. Sophia, a music lover, went to the rehearsal and pronounced the performance very good. The concert was billed in the printed programs as "Verdi's Requiem in Honor of Arthur Yale Lodge."

Friends beseeched her for days to add to the eulogy before the concert. "There will not be a eulogy, not a word from anyone." She despised the speeches of ministers and priests, who did not know the deceased, telling their generic platitudes. Even worse were the tear-choked reminiscences of family who remembered that "Gramps was always called Grumpy" or the amusing story of "old Eve losing her dentures before the party" or the boredom of hearing sainthood conferred upon old Joe by his weeping widow. No, Leda decided, not a word. Let everyone remember what there was to remember privately—silence. It was all over.

In the front orchestra section of Carnegie Hall, set aside for family and friends. Leda, dressed in black sat in the front row next to an enlarged picture of Arthur and massive bouquets of white roses. A free concert had great appeal and the rest of the seats were completely full. The performance ended to thunderous applause. Leda stood in line to accept the condolences of many people that she knew and did not know.

After the concert, Leda, Leslie and Sophia went out to eat at Trattoria della Arte near Carnegie Hall. They all ordered much and ate little discussing the concert and the people who attended. Leda's total consumption was three vodkas and a plate of veal piccata cooling beside her. "What will you do now?" practical Leslie asked.

"Go back to Damascus," was her instinctive reply.

"Leda, you are crazy!" Sophia almost toppled her red wine with an extravagant gesture.

"There is really nothing for me here and my work at the refugee camps is yet to be done. I had only spent one day there when I was called back."

"But you must put your life in order, you need time to grieve," Leslie explained while finishing the last of her mussels.

"My life is over, in order or chaos, so I may as well be of use to someone. Rhoda will live in the house temporarily and see that bills are paid and my animals cared for. Anyway, I will only stay three months with Aliyah and that should give me time to lose myself in something constructive instead of just brooding and crying. But there is still life here," continued Leda, "Do tell me what is going on with you."

Sophia taking a sip of wine said, "Well, I don't want to burden you with my problems at a time like this, but I feel that you will know soon enough anyway. Conrad is having an affair and has left me. Apparently, all that I had done with my life to please him did not make him happy. His nurse at the office is pregnant. She is 20 years younger. So you see, we are both widows in a way, but I prefer your fate," said Sophia. "Arthur did not leave you willingly but Conrad chose to leave me for someone else. You were not rejected Leda."

The three friends had a moment of silence as if to commemorate the dead marriage. Then Sophia, embarrassed, said, "Leslie, tell us more about your brilliant career." and Leslie went into a discussion of her latest career triumph as the CEO of Gainer, the largest polling company in the country.

"I have always thought that those polls are rigged. They are based on phone calls and who answers the phone at home these days?" Leda pronounced and ended the discussion.

Leda told them about her work, about Aliyah and mentioned Talib. Just saying his name out loud to her friends was confusing and somehow shameful causing her to stop talking and take a sip of water.

The lunch ended and the limousine took them back to Leda's house where they packed and left for their homes. "Don't go back, Leda. Stay here. You really aren't emotionally ready to undertake anything challenging. You know war with Iraq is imminent. Arthur would not let you go," Leslie made her case as she was going through the door.

Silence. Blessed silence. Leda went to her study and looked at the stack of bills, called her broker and told him to sell some stocks. The broker told her it was not a good idea but Leda was insistent. The one thing she had never expected had happened – a Black Swan event. This book by Nassim Taleb discussed risk and the occurrence of the unexpected. Arthur's death was not in her life plan and now she must make a life around it. *But do I want to live it?*

She picked up the phone and called Aliyah. "Thank you for the flowers. You knew white roses indicate sorrow."

"Leda, we were devastated by the news and I so wish I could have been with you."

"I know of all your efforts to come to the funeral but understand that visas for Syrians to come to America are almost impossible to get."

"I am making reservations to return to Damascus. I know that I have not been in touch with you but there was so much…"

"But I didn't think that you would be returning. I think Talib called you to tell you that we will be working in the West Bank."

Leda remembered the unanswered calls "I must have missed the message but absolutely want to continue."

"If you want to come, make arrangements through to Tel Aviv and I will meet you." Aliyah continued, "I will arrange for your papers."

"I am coming," said a determined Leda.

CHAPTER 12

Leda was halted on arrival at the luxurious and modern Tel Aviv Ben-Gurion airport. Since her passport carried the Syrian stamp, Israeli officials questioned her trip, denied her a tourist visa, and returned her to Paris. She called New York and talked to her friend Larry Aronson who was on the board of UNWRA - United Nations Works and Relief Agency, in charge of Palestinians. He was more than glad to process her request to make her an UNWRA observer. He faxed the necessary documents and she was delayed in Paris for only three days until she got back on the plane to Tel Aviv.

Aliyah met her at arrivals and once again offered her sympathy on the loss of her husband. "Leda, you should not have come. You need your own familiar surroundings to deal with your grief. You are just running away from reality here."

Walking through the airport, Leda stopped, turned, and with a stricken expression said, "I couldn't stay in that house with all those memories. At least here the suffering is so real I can taste it and it puts my grief into context. Whenever I have been depressed, I read about World War I. The thought of the trenches at Verdun and the slaughter at Gallipoli always has the power to put my problems into context. The world is such a brutal and painful place but there are degrees of insanity and only by focusing on the ultimate in grief do I get perspective and find peace for my private sorrows." Aliyah hugged her and gave her a tissue to wipe away her tears.

A driver took Leda's bags and led her to a small van. As they drove through Tel Aviv, she saw a beautiful modern city on the banks of the Mediterranean. They passed skyscrapers, the King David Hilton and luxurious shops. She knew that they were going straight to Jerusalem and, therefore, although she was fatigued, she tried to discern as much as she could about this city. She was surprised to see so many people from the Philippines on the streets. "Oh yes," said Aliyah, "there are 300,000 as household workers because most Israelis are afraid to let Palestinians into their homes even though Palestinians unemployment is over 60%."

On the road to Jerusalem, Leda was aware of the desolate landscape, the rocky hills devoid of greenery and the parched look of the land. It was very ugly country. "We will be working in the West Bank, and it will be more dangerous than in Syria because of the constant conflict between the Israelis and the Palestinians. You were very smart to contact UNWRA because the Israelis have a good opinion of the organization. You must be very careful here. The Israelis are very sensitive about any publicity regarding their treatment of the Palestinians."

"I am not a child. I know this is a difficult situation, but I must help the Palestinians."

"As an American, you will also be the target of some fanatical Palestinians who have sixty years of pent up anger against the West. They feel their land was stolen, their people mistreated and humiliated and they see America as a friend of Israel and endorser of this brutality. They will not stop to ask for your personal philosophy before they try to kill you."

Leda smiled as if to brush away Aliyah's warning. "How can they kill me? I am already more than half-dead. My life was over when Arthur died. A swift death of martyrdom would be welcome."

Aliyah gasped at this idea and squeezed Leda's hand. "You need to heal, my dear, you are a walking wound."

After several hours, they arrived in Jerusalem, an old city of a quarter of a million inhabitants with a completely different look than Tel Aviv. They drove around the city walls enclosing the most ancient part of Jerusalem.

"This wall encloses four sections: Jewish, Arab, Christian and Armenian. This citadel encloses all the religions with a common base in Abraham" explained Aliyah. "Here is our hotel, The American Colony. We are in East Jerusalem, the Arab half of the city. You will be pleased Leda, it is a very luxurious hotel left over from the British occupation of Palestine."

Entering she observed the thick walls, polished stone floors and outdoor courtyards- a testament to the days of empire and aristocracy. Leda was happy to have this as home base for the next few months. "Journalists and scholars meet in the bar every evening and this is where Tony Blair has an apartment when he is trying to work out peace" commented the bellboy showing them to their quarters. "We were here first say the Jews, but you have not owned it for the last three thousand years say the Arabs."

Through their window they could see the Dome of the Rock, built on the Temple Mount. The bellboy continued, "This glistening dome is the source of bitter contention between the Jews to whom it is the site of Solomon's Temple and the Arabs who consider it the site where Mohammed ascended into heaven." *What passion over land,-God as a real estate agent answering the prayers of two peoples who wanted to occupy the same space.*

The next day at the Wailing Wall or, as the Israeli guide corrected her, the Western Wall; she saw hundreds of Jews with their Yarmulkes and prayer shawls bobbing their heads up and down praying. "The Jews only have this piece of the original Temple and wail and cry because of the sadness over its destruction. The women are on one side and the men at the other in this huge open air synagogue."

This two thousand year passion for the rebuilding of the Temple and the return to Greater Israel's original land area in 1200 BC was evident here. A return to Solomon's days of glory was the motivating force of Zionism. Was God a racist? Is that why he called the Jews His chosen people?

The important Christian sites were next on her agenda. On the Via Dolorosa, basically a path in the middle of shops with haggling vendors, she saw priests with their pilgrims saying the Rosary out loud while being harassed by the merchants on both sides. The sight was nauseating. This most holy place, considered to be the final path of Christ dragging the cross in His agony, turned into a commercial spectacle. The church to mark the Crucifixion was overdone and overfilled with the overwrought. Leda did not find any religious or spiritual meaning in this hodge-podge.

God is not present here at least not any God that I understand. God is more real in the silence of an open field or the wonder of a starry sky. He could not be here, there's too much noise.

The next morning Aliyah and Leda set out for the refugee camp. On the way there, she noticed that they were leaving Jerusalem on a big highway and there was a small, winding road to their side with different license plates. Aliyah explained that only cars with Israeli license plates could travel the highways, the Palestinians had to use their own roads that had checkpoints. *This marked the Palestinians with license plates just as the Jews were marked with yellow armbands in Nazi Germany.* Because of Leda's UNWRA status, they were able to use the highways meant for the Israelis, so it was an easy trip from the American Colony.

Arriving, Leda was introduced to the clinic, which due to funding from UNRWA was tolerable. The routine of driving out to the refugee camps and working until nightfall began and to be in this luxurious hotel after her days at the camp was a blessing. She developed a collegial camaraderie with Ali her assistant and she sensed the beginnings of teamwork.

In the clinic and the hotel she heard many stories of Israeli atrocities—of buildings demolished; of acquisition of Palestinian private property; of children shot for hurling stones; of people imprisoned without due process; of the degradation of multiple checkpoints and the nightmare of multiple permits- for travel, building, buying. For a Palestinian to build a house requires an eight-year wait for permits. The Red Crescent, the Islamic Red Cross, was routinely denied access to critically injured people.

This is like Germany in 1939. Were there any good souls who helped the Jews in that debacle? A few, but not many. In 1939 I would have been first to help the Jews against their German murderers. I definitely get the sense that the Israelis are treating the Palestinians as the Germans had treated them. They expertly learned how to deal with "sub-humans" from their own experiences.

Journalists, UN workers and Israeli intellectuals held court in the bar in the evenings. "Two -state solution, impossible!" stated Ari, a right wing journalist, "We gave them Gaza, and what do they do? They bomb Israel."

"Professor Isaacs retorted, "The deplorable treatment of Palestinians and hampering the two state solution by constant building of settlements will be fatal to Israel. They will either become one state which due to the rapid birth rate of the Palestinians will give them a majority or they will become an apartheid state like South Africa and deserve the condemnation of the world."

"There is a third solution," piped up Nate, a blogger, "some think that all the Palestinians should be in Jordan."

"Never, that would be ethnic cleansing" said Leda in horror.

The lively discussion broke up, as ever, with no conclusions. *Discussions like this would be considered anti-Semitic back home.*

Hard work filled Leda's days and she found reprieve from her heartache. She felt Arthur's spirit approving her altruistic actions. She would spend the next few months working here and then return home. But to what? An empty life? A gradual slow decline into senility? Tired as she was after her long days her future tortured her during her anguished nights.

CHAPTER 15

With still no sign of Talib, Leda finally asked Aliyah about him. "Why yes, Leda. We spoke about you several times. He had asked me extensively about your background before you even arrived and has followed the details of your visit." Aliyah then took Leda's arm and said earnestly, "Leda, please do not get too friendly with him. I must warn you, Talib is involved in activities that are of interest to the Mossad. For me, it is nothing. But for you, as an American citizen, there can be severe repercussions."

So he is interested in me? What danger could there be in that? Leda smiled.

Rapidly Leda became adept at doing the type of medicine she had not done since medical school. She became expert at gunshot wounds and removal of bomb shrapnel fragments inflicted by the constant skirmishes. High fevers, fractures, burns, dysentery, and advanced cancers kept her days busy. Nights were spent in study of the latest treatments on the Internet.

She was either too busy or too tired to grieve during daylight hours. However, at night, in bed, there were moments of brutal awakening to the reality that she was alone. The bell jar of exclusion from the rest of humanity descended upon her and she felt unloved and isolated. Arthur had been her main conduit to love and life and without him she was enveloped in a shroud of emotional indifference. Whenever she thought of life with Arthur it seemed distant, as if it were a fantasy.

Her work was approaching an end when one morning an alarm went up at the camp. It was a hideous, shrill scream of danger. A Red Crescent ambulance drove into the compound throwing up dust in its wake. An Israeli bomb had hit a Palestinian village in retaliation for a suicide bomber, and the Israelis would not let the ambulance into a Jerusalem hospital, so the driver had to come miles to this clinic.

Leda threw open the door and saw a mass of people one on top of another moaning and screaming in a sea of blood. She had opened a door on a human abattoir. With Ali's help, she dragged out the bodies and triaged according to their condition. After removing about 13 people, Leda pronounced half of them dead from loss of blood or the severity of their wounds. She noticed in a far corner a woman with a bleeding head wound holding on to a tiny girl who had her eyes shut and was screaming. As Leda and Ali lifted the woman, she begged, "Please take care of my little Yasmin," in perfect English before she lost consciousness.

An hour later a second Red Crescent ambulance arrived and Leda saw that most bodies were no longer moving. The driver, with a red face and tears streaming down his cheeks, said they were held up at a checkpoint. Ali explained that by delaying medical care, the Israeli hope was that the Palestinian death toll would go up. After all, could severely hurt people survive an hour ride through primitive desert roads and an hour-long checkpoint? There were ten dead with two on the brink of death.

Leda did not go home that night and the crash course in trauma would come back to haunt the rest of her life. She had seen gruesome scenes before but never on this scale. Blood was the canvas and on it there were missing limbs, glistening stomach intestines, parts of faces with hunks of hair. The sound track was of screaming which drowned out the worst sound - the agony of moaning.

These horrific scenes will come back to stalk me. I got a permanent tattoo on my life today. It will always be with me to torment me. She did not sleep that night but had a cigarette with Ali as dawn was breaking. "How do you erase these scenes from your mind?"

Ali put down his cigarette, "What you observe is always part of you. The trick is to also have joy and good to focus on."

"The panorama of today's hell will always outweigh any good I have seen in my life."

The morning brought more help from the city and quite a few reporters from Al Jazeera, the Arabic news service. But, of course, there were no news services from the western world and only one line, "In retaliation for a suicide bombing, the Israeli army bombed the village of Nerus, near Hebron, where terrorists were thought to be hiding." There was no mention of the casualties or the prevention of the ambulances from reaching a hospital.

She looked over at Leila's bed and asked Ali, "Who is

taking care of the little girl? She seems to be sleeping by her mother's side."

"If you want I could bring her some milk from the canteen."

Ali gave the milk to Leda who woke the little girl and tried to get her to drink. She took a few sips and as she looked up at Leda, she started to cry. Leda took her in her arms and the child cried louder. *I was never any good with children. This injured woman with the small child caught up in such an inhuman situation.*

Leda was told the mother's name was Leile al Karim and realized that she was the most beautiful woman she had ever seen. Bandages soaked in blood covered one injured eye but the remaining eye was like an emerald shielded by the longest lashes Leda had ever seen. Leile's hair was long, thick and shiny and her features were classic. Leile's condition was critical and she was drifting in and out of consciousness. In addition to the head wound, she suffered internal injuries by shielding her daughter's body from a collapsed roof beam.

"Why did this happen to her? How was she involved?"

A young man with a missing arm answered. "Leile's husband was the suicide bomber who killed five people and wounded twenty on a bus in Jerusalem. In retaliation, the Israel Defense Forces bombed our village."

"We cannot help her here. She needs major surgery. Ali, we need to transfer her to a fully equipped hospital!"

"The nearest good hospital is in Jerusalem but multiple documents are necessary for Palestinians to enter Jerusalem," explained Ali. "Just to pass a checkpoint the documents are checked three times after a long wait. No cars are allowed across checkpoints so Leile would need transfer from one ambulance to another at each checkpoint. And the most difficult feat is to be allowed into Jerusalem. It will require a miracle to take Leile there."

Leda, after 28 hours, went home. *I will do everything to get Leile's transfer to a Jerusalem hospital.*

Aliyah was aghast when she saw Leda enter the American Colony unkempt and covered in blood. Leda quickly explained the situation to Aliyah and promised to pay for any medical care required, as long as she could do something for Leile. "Please, Aliyah, call and see what could be done!" pleaded Leda as she went to take a shower. To save Leile was Leda's latest cause. *Why this desperate connection with an unknown woman?*

Leile was beautiful and her beauty made her a counterweight among all the misery around her. Beauty was rare, fragile, and priceless – an attribute to be honored and preserved- especially valuable in this sea of ugliness.

The morning brought a wave of helplessness as Aliyah explained, "The Israeli government hesitates to let any Palestinian refugees out of the camps into Jerusalem and especially refuses to give permission to anyone with a terrorist in the family. The idea of getting documents for the wife of a terrorist is impossible."

"Aliyah, for the love of God, we must help," pleaded Leda. "Does the will of God become evident in the circumstances that are thrown in our path of life? I cannot calm the Middle East or bring justice for Palestine. But I can help this one woman."

Leda called the American Embassy in Tel Aviv and spoke

with Ambassador Neil Hobbes. She explained the situation and begged for help in convincing the Israeli officials to issue permission for hospital transport for one Palestinian woman. Mr. Hobbes was very sympathetic but at the end said that the official American policy was not to interfere in any way in matters concerning the Palestinians because this may upset American-Israeli relations. Leda put down the phone with a feeling of utter helplessness. The pit of hopelessness sparked the flame of disgust and revulsion at the official American policy. When she considered the reason she was given, her mind burst into a screeching storm of anger and desire for revenge.

Where was justice? Where was the America she had loved and admired for bringing justice and freedom to the world? She had upheld all American military conflicts because she believed that they were right. In World War I America fought unjust aggression, In World War II she helped destroy the evil of Nazi domination, in the Korean War she fought the plague of Communism. And now America was in league with an oppressor. She had despised the Viet Nam protestors because they stood against the true blue principles of the United States. Perhaps she was also deluded then? What justice could she expect from a government that was responsible for Arthur's death?

She decided to call on the only other possibility, Lord Denver, who was visiting Tel Aviv from Damascus at the British Embassy. She knew of Lord Denver's obvious fascination with Aliyah and was ready to take advantage. Leda had Aliyah's driver take her to Tel Aviv after placing a call and asking for an emergency appointment.

The British embassy was in an impressive building.

Two soldiers stood outside with machine guns over their shoulders. A small British flag was flying. The surrounding stonewall was filled with graffiti, FUCK YOU, BRITISH GO HOME. She wondered what the American Embassy looked like. She presented her documents and entered the heavy carved door. A man in a dark suit led her over marble floors into a salon with tall ceilings and English style furniture. A portrait of Queen Elizabeth II graced a wall. A photograph of the large-eared Tony Blair, autographed "to my dear friend, Lord Denver" stood on the console. Ruminating on the decline of the British Empire, Leda gained courage.

"My dear Dr. Eimont, to what do I owe this pleasure," said Lord Denver entering the room. "I was told that it was an emergency. Dear, dear," he murmured shaking his head. His soft little hand took Leda's. "Shall we have coffee?" he inquired as he showed her to a rose satin covered sofa.

Leda took a deep breath and launched in, "Lord Denver, I plead with you to help me. There is a Palestinian woman in critical condition because she could not get emergency treatment. First, by the Israelis who refused to let an ambulance through the checkpoints, and now because of red tape regarding the movement of Palestinians into Jerusalem. Could you help me and intervene on my behalf with the authorities?"

"I am so sorry, but this is a matter that we do not delve in. I have been asked this on occasion and my Embassy has an official position not to intervene in internal affairs." said Lord Denver sadly, as he lowered his eyes to avoid Leda's stare.

Leda jumped up in outrage. "Have you no humanity! Have you no guts!

Lord Denver, a meek and withdrawn person, was shocked. "Dear, dear," he mumbled as his eyes widened with surprise. "You must really feel very strongly about this person. We are quite immune to Israeli atrocities. They always claim it is retaliation for bombing, but we all see the horrific concentration camp conditions the Palestinians live in and that suicide bombing is their only retort. They consider themselves freedom fighters and the Palestinians designate them martyrs. But my dear, this is so prevalent. Eventually, you will see, the Israelis will win with all of the American money and weaponry behind them. They will occupy the entire territory of Palestine and if there are any Palestinians left, they will form reservations where they will be confined. You know, just like the Native American Indians, defeated by a superior strength."

Leda was looking at him in disbelief. "And you condone this outrage? There is a crime against humanity occurring and everyone turns away! We are not among uncivilized barbarians but among the most educated, the brightest of people in the world and we all pretend that all is OK?"

Lord Denver looked at her and said, "It is only the truth of Darwin's theory - the survival of the fittest." A large silver cat entered the room and climbed on Lord Denver's lap. A woman over six-foot tall with silver hair soon entered. Her face was attractive but she must have been twice as big as Lord Denver.

"Tasha, come here, you bad kitty!" she called and looking over at Leda she said, "I am so sorry to disturb you."

"Why Dr. Eimont, it gives me pleasure to introduce you at last to my wife, Lady Denver." As Leda rose to greet

Lady Denver, Lord Denver explained the nature of Leda's request.

"You must not get involved with these primitive people. They live in such archaic conditions, have such strange beliefs and are so violent that they are hardly civilized. What they are doing to the poor Israelis is a crime. After all, the Jews have a homeland given to them by God and now these poor people have to die to claim it."

"Dr. Eimont, there is something I could do, for you and Aliyah." At that moment Leda realized the depth of feeling that Lord Denver had for her friend. He would risk something not for the Palestinians or Leda, but because he wanted to be a hero in Aliyah's eyes. "The only one who could possibly help you is Francois Bayrou, the French Ambassador. I will give him a call and plead your cause." An appointment in hand, she bid Lord Denver goodbye and promised to convey his dearest greetings to Aliyah.

The French Embassy also had guards and people lined up seeking visas. She presented her documents and was led right in. The interior was less grand and had the appearance of a huge government office. She was led to a modern office and the skinny, tall man with mussed blond man at the desk looked startled to see her. "You are here already! Madam, you must have taken a jet!" He smiled at her. "I understand- a humanitarian concern. I usually count out my requests to the Israeli government like bottles of water in the desert. I want to have enough for the really death defying moments. However, this will be one of them, not because of you Madam or your cause, but because Lord Denver has never once asked me to intervene. It is important to be owed a favor by the British, eh?" He winked at Leda.

He picked up a phone and, speaking in fluent Arabic, pursued a discussion of many tones and inflections. "A messenger will bring you the permission slip later this afternoon. You are truly a powerful woman with the British."

"Thank you so very much, merci beaucoup! French gallantry is still alive." *The entire matter of Leile's life had hinged on the inexplicable crush that little Lord Denver had for the lovely Aliyah.*

CHAPTER 14

The documents had been delivered to the hotel, so Leda and Aliyah took Leile and Yasmin to Jerusalem. The hospital there compared with the best in America. Orderlies took Leile into surgery immediately, and Yasmin was crying as Leda took her into her arms. The little girl clung to her fiercely. "Aliyah, there is no place here for the child, we will get a cot in my room at the hotel and get a woman to take care of it."

Aliyah smiled as Leda called the child "it." Now this was the true Leda. Children had no role in her life. "Yes, Leda, let's take her to the hotel until her mother recovers."

Returning, Aliyah warmed some milk in the hotel kitchen and stirred in some eggs and sugar. As Yasmin was eating, her whole little body shook with the desperation: the child was starving. Finally, she washed her in some warm, soapy water and dressed her in a soft blouse. Pulling in a bed from another room, placing it in Leda's room, and making a makeshift crib out of pillows seemed like child's play. Yasmin was asleep before she even covered her with a warm blanket.

Leile's chest operation was a success. Her spleen was removed, but she had extensive liver damage so her prognosis was still in doubt. At least she was alive. Leda examined Leile's wounded eye and decided to operate to remove the foreign body. Leda fell into her stride during the operation, "scalpel, sponge, retract" the words of her specialty were familiar and the assistant was a doctor trained in the States, glad to be working with the famous Dr. Eimont. The surgery finished, Leda knew that there was a good chance of having vision restored in that beautiful eye with the emerald green iris. Leda knew enough plastic surgery to suture the eyelid. *At least my part of Leile's recovery will be fine.*

Every day after work Leda went to visit Leile to see her progress. "How can I ever thank you for your splendid miracle? To be in this amazing hospital you must have moved mountains. But most of all I am grateful for your care of Yasmin, I can see she is cared for."

"Leile, Yasmin will be fine. Do not worry. I am sorry to see this situation with so much pain. I was told the bombing was in retaliation for a suicide bombing in Jerusalem."

"Doctor, the suicide bomber was my husband, Abu." Leile said in a very low voice.

"I am trying to understand, why was your husband a suicide bomber?"

Leile looked away before she sadly looked at Leda, "You come from a different world but you feel compassion so it should not be difficult for you to understand him."

She pushed herself up on her pillows, took Leda's hand

and started hesitantly, "Abu's family owned olive groves for generations and was well off. My parents worked on the land and, in return, got a house, a plot of land and a portion of the olive harvest. I married Abu, had loved him from childhood. Israeli settlers came and asked us to leave the land. We refused. Then Israeli soldiers cut down our olive trees. We still tried to live on the land but it became harder and harder to grow food. We moved in with some poor relatives in the adjacent village—all seven of us in a one room hut. We had still hoped to return to our olive grove. One day as I was walking by, I saw an Israeli couple with several workers and huge construction machinery building houses on our land!" Leile was crying and Leda noticed with alarm that her eye bandage was becoming tinged with blood.

"But the government must have compensated you for your land!" Leda stated in outrage as she changed the bandage.

"No, there was no compensation. They believe they are entitled by God to all of Palestine" After a pause, she continued, "Abu looked for work but found none. The unemployment rate is over 60 percent. He tried to find work in Israel for two dollars a day cleaning the streets. There were up to three checkpoints that had to be passed in order to reach work." Here Leile let out a deep sigh. "The Israeli soldiers would goad the people waiting, and the lines would grow longer and longer. Gaza and Hebron are completely separated from each other and the Palestinian lands have no common borders with anyone except Israel, so the Israeli government holds Palestinians in a vise. There is no freedom for Palestinians to travel to jobs, or schools, or hospitals because all is controlled by Israeli checkpoints." Leile said with a resigned look.

"In the last 4 months in my village the curfew was only lifted for a total of 82 hours. This means we must be in our homes with very limited opportunity to go outside, seek medical help, or buy groceries. We are in a prison and the whole world turns its face. One third of our children suffer from chronic malnutrition. This year they have not been able to go to school at all due to the harsh methods of Ariel Sharon." Leile turned and winced with pain. "Some men in the village tried to protest but the Israeli soldiers came in the middle of the night, arrested them and they have not been heard of since."

"I find this so hard to believe. This is against international law, against humanity. If things were this bad, we would have read about it in our news, it would be on television," an exasperated Leda said.

"My son Ibrahim was 9 years old and he had seen all this happen," continued Leile with a hushed voice. "One day he went with some older boys and threw rocks at the soldiers. They returned the rocks with gunfire and my little boy was shot in the chest. Dr. Eimont there is no pain greater for a mother than to see her child suffering." Leda felt Leile's nails digging into her hand. "I ran to the soldiers for help. I asked them for transport to a hospital but they pushed me away with their guns. I took a wheelbarrow and my husband and I ran two miles with my bleeding boy to the nearest border. There was a line of people waiting for inspection, but when they saw the bleeding boy, they stepped aside to let us pass.

The guards said that the wrong documents had been brought and that my husband should return home to find the proper documents. There was no hope. My husband returned, wet with tears and sweat, but it was too late. My son was dead. It was at that moment that my husband decided to become a suicide bomber. He could not just forgive and forget."

Leda's eyes filled with tears as she visualized the progression of Leile's story. "I understand what made your husband act but you must calm yourself and get some sleep. We will talk tomorrow." Leda bent down and kissed Leile on the forehead.

Aliyah met her at the door; "I spoke with Talib and told him that today was a particularly hard day for you. He said you need to relax and I should order you a drink." A few minutes later a knock on their door produced a waiter with a tray. Leda gratefully took the ice cold Martini, drank it down, and recounted Leila's story. She asked Aliyah, "Can it really be true, all that I heard today?"

Aliyah put down a plate of olives and replied, "I am sure the story you heard was true, but you know there are two sides to every story and the suicide bomber who blew up a bus with many people is not loved by the Israelis."

"This is war then- a true war, but an undeclared war—a war in which the Israelis have all the weapons, rifles, helicopters, and a full-fledged army. They do not use military attack because they would be using them against a population whose only weapons are rocks and their bodies ringed with explosives. So they destroy their enemy, the Palestinians, by slow torture and when the crisis reaches a boiling point and leads the Palestinians to retaliate, they are called terrorists.

Of course, going after terrorists legitimizes the use of the Army."

"How can you call this a war when the target is innocent Israeli citizens, not the Army?"

"How can boys with rocks or men whose only weapon is their body fight an army? So they choose the only target available—civilians. The last war where more armed men were killed than civilians was World War I; after that, in all wars increasing numbers of civilians were killed. After all who was killed in Nagasaki, in Dresden? Civilians."

"We will not solve the problems of the Middle East tonight. By the way, Yasmin is an entertaining little girl. The maid takes her to a small room by the kitchen during the day and the little one plays with the pots and pans. She is so thin. I bought her a few clothes. She has not had much to eat lately. Tomorrow I will take her to the hospital and give her all the vaccinations. I really don't think she's had any medical care."

"Let me see her," Leda said as Aliyah followed her to her room. Through the open door they saw a little, dark, curly-haired child sleeping. "She looks just like a kitten." Aliyah smiled as she thought that Leda was fond of this child since she related it to a small animal that she liked.

The next morning Leda arrived at the hospital to find Leile sleeping. *Leile's complexion is yellow – not a good sign – it means her liver is failing.* As she was examining her Leile woke with a smile, "I saw my Yasmin today because Aliyah was kind enough to bring her," said the patient. "Yasmin was not happy since she had injections and vaccinations from Dr. Aliyah. Now that I no longer have my husband or son, Yasmin is my only consolation." Leile looked at Leda and said, "You are a very kind lady to come here from America to help us especially when I heard from Aliyah that you had just lost your husband."

"Yes, he died suddenly. He was the great love of my life."

"And you do not have children? In our culture it is very sad when a woman does not have children. We have prayers and rituals to beg God for children so that we would not be barren."

Barren. Is that what she was? No! She did not walk about with a big void where the womb should be. I am a thoroughbred, not a brood mare. I have no desire to replicate myself- I am an original.

Her thoughts were interrupted by Leile saying "...and so after not sleeping for many nights my husband said that with the loss of his son he no longer wanted to live. I was beside myself with sorrow—losing my son, and then, facing the loss of my husband. The cruelty of my son's death was like an open wound, constantly bleeding, constantly spewing an agony of pain."

"Did you know that he was planning to be a suicide bomber?"

"No, I could tell that he was saying goodbye by the tenderness he showed to me and Yasmin. One day he said that Allah would be with us and not to forget him. That was the last time I saw him."

Leile was having a problem continuing and Leda gave her a sip of water. "I heard that there had been a suicide bombing in Jerusalem. The Israelis did not know where he came from, only that he got on a bus in Jerusalem and exploded himself and killed five people and wounded twenty. When he did not come home that night, I knew in my heart that it was him. The next day, this article appeared in a Palestinian newspaper." Leile reached into her small bag by the bedside and pulled out a tattered article. As she glanced at the article, Leda remembered the retaliation, directed at the usual suspect, the Janin refugee camp. She remembered reading the account. Now here it was again. Leda asked an English-speaking nurse to read the article in Arabic and to translate it for her in English.

> *"The Israeli Occupation Forces made the bottom of the camp into a closed military zone using twelve tanks, ten jeeps, and at least two Apache helicopters. A woman, a Palestinian journalist, had been trying to get between unarmed children and the tanks. She was arrested and taken to a place where about twenty Palestinian men were held blindfolded, handcuffed, stripped to their underwear and beaten. After being interrogated, she was free to go. She asked to stay with the men, to minimize the violence, but she was dragged away. A UN worker, waving a blue UN flag, negotiated with the soldiers for the children to go home. The soldier's response was broadcast in English, "We don't care if you are the United Nations or who you are. Fuck off and go home!" The UN worker said this is what they were trying to do.*

The Palestinian journalist headed home and on the way a group of children told her that a ten-year old, Muhammad Ali, had been killed and three children had been wounded by tank fire. She walked to where the tanks were firing on them erratically. When she was about 50 meters from the tanks she implored them not to shoot live ammunition at unarmed children.

"What about Jerusalem yesterday! What about those children?!" shouted a soldier. The woman answered, "These children here were not the ones who did that." Then, they held their fire.

An armed personnel carrier drove up and a soldier began shooting into the air and most of the children dispersed. Three small children remained and the woman tried to get them into the alley. A soldier pointed a gun at her and shot her in the thigh as she crawled up the alley. She was carried to the Emergency Room of Janin Hospital where she saw the UN worker brought in. The Israeli army prohibited a clearly marked UN ambulance from evacuating him for nearly one hour, during which time he lost blood and died."

The nurse turned to Leda and said, "This was retaliation for what had not even done by someone in Janin. It was only later that they uncovered the truth and bombed Leile's village. The Israeli Defense Forces engage in a shoot to kill policy. The lack of accountability on Israel's part has become bolder as the events described become almost standard. These are not military campaigns. They are acts of terror designed to humiliate, brutalize, and bully Palestinians into subjugation. They are being denied not only the right to resist but also the right to exist."

"But what about the press, certainly they would pick up a story about a UN worker killed by the Israelis." exclaimed Leda

The nurse looked at Leda and said, "Quote –*The New York Times*- '*During a skirmish at Jenin Refugee Camp, a UN worker was killed.*' This makes it sound as if the Palestinians did it." She grimaced as she turned on her heel and left.

Leda looked over at Leile. She looked more jaundiced than ever. Leile was dying and speaking very softly. "So you see, my darling husband not only retaliated in Jerusalem but he was also responsible for the whole tragedy at Jenin. It took a week, but finally under torture, they identified my husband as the suicide bomber. It was then that they bombed us. Then the bulldozers demolished everything in our small village—only five homes, but it was shelter to twenty-six of us. The cycle of sadness, will it ever end? And now my little Yasmin. I know you did your best but I know I am dying." Leile's last request was to see her little Yasmin one more time.

Leda knew that a psychological will to live was sometimes the most important factor. That afternoon Leda brought Yasmin to see her mother. "I knew you would enjoy this visit."

The little girl jumped on her mother's bed, oblivious to her wincing in pain.

"Promise me, Dr. Eimont, because you are the kindest person I ever met, please promise me you will find a home for my little Yasmin. I am sure she does not need much. She is a good child. Please let her stay with me this evening. Perhaps Allah will allow me to live for her."

The next morning as Leda returned to the clinic anxious to see how Leile was doing, her worst fears were confirmed when she saw the white, staring, open-mouthed face. The little girl still huddled in the dead woman's arms clinging to the rapidly cooling body. Leda closed Leile's lids and knelt down. She started to pray to the Virgin Mary, to Christ, to Mohammed, to God, to any power that could remove this horrible cycle of death and destruction from this life so intrinsically cruel, unjust and brutal. How can people rejoice at a newborn child? Do they do so in ignorance or a mindless optimism that through a miraculous change in circumstances this child's life will be free of disappointments, pain, sickness and death?

Leda took Yasmin back to the hotel and left the child with the maid in her room. She had a sad and quiet dinner with Aliyah in the courtyard restaurant. As Leda related Leila's story, Aliyah received a call from Talib.

"I must get back to Damascus immediately." Aliyah said after her long conversation in Arabic. Leda sensed that Aliyah would not reveal what was happening or the reason for her rapid departure.

"I want to spend a few more weeks at the camp hospital.

Yasmin must be prepared for her mother's death and then what will I do with her?"

"Leda, Yasmin will survive. Besides, I got the name of a good orphanage where you could leave her in Ramallah. I already contacted them and when you leave in a few weeks, please take her there. It will be an adequate life for the child." The women returned to their rooms where Aliyah started packing but stopped when she saw Yasmin.

The child was two years old: dark curly hair, a café au lait complexion, small hands with dirty little fingernails, and thin, slight body except for the rosy cheeks. Aliyah spoke softly in Arabic to her about her mother's death. Leda bent to pick her up and the most pitiful shriek and a pouring of voluminous tears seemed to spring from a vast hidden well. Leda found herself crying.

The next two weeks Leda enjoyed the hugs that waited for her at the end of her long days. She started to become attached to the little one and wanted to insure her safety and happiness. She bought treats for Yasmin and was rewarded by tiny kisses. She decided that she would pay for the child's care and later for her tuition. With financial help the child could be assured of a good future.

Leda kept putting off the day when they would take her to the orphanage. One day Leda returned to find Yasmin's room empty and felt a void, emptiness. "Where is Yasmin?" she asked Ali.

"Dr. Eimont, I know it was a difficult chore for you so I spoke with Dr. Aliyah and drove Yasmin to Ramallah myself. All is fine, she is at home in the orphanage."

CHAPTER 15

In the Damascus twilight Aliyah met the car she had sent to Jerusalem for Leda. She gasped as the door opened to reveal Leda holding the child. "Leda! What have you done? Yasmin should be in the orphanage in Ramallah!"

"Has she been fed?" Aliyah asked with motherly concern as she called a maid to prepare a room for the child.

The two women went to the silk sofa in the library. Aliyah looked up and said, "If not an orphanage, you should leave Yasmin with her family. I am sure that a relative will take care of her. Palestinians have a tradition of caring for their extended family members."

Leda pacing the room in turmoil was dying for a drink. "Would it be impolite of me to ask you for a drink of whiskey?"

"Of course you may have some," Aliyah answered as she went to a cabinet and poured some Laphroig into a crystal glass. Leda sipped the smoky, strong drink. "Leda, answer me about the child. You treat this incident as if you had brought home a stray kitten. She is not a pet. She is a human being who somehow fell into your hands," Aliyah said with some force of emotion. "Why did you bring her here? Do you intend to take her home?"

"I must ask you to let me keep this child here until I find someplace to put her. When I left Jerusalem I went to the orphanage in Ramallah to see how Yasmin was doing. The conditions there were horrible!"

These questions brought into play all her thoughts and feelings about progeny since she herself was very young. *It is my conviction that the cycle of life is just that—cyclical—and all the dreams and aspirations people put into the new generation are almost always foiled. The human animal, although advertised as the new and improved model, turns out not to be necessarily so.*

Leda went to see Yasmin playing with a little doll in her room. What is Yasmin's future? Is there any hope for her? Did Leile consider this fate, these unbearable conditions, when she had her?

So what was the purpose of procreation? Some people loved the activity of raising children as an occupation. But it was hardly a necessity with over seven billion in production. The more people, the more problems as any Malthusian would be apt to point out. In the big scheme of things, and contrary to the idea of the sanctity of human life, human life is probably one of the cheapest commodities on the face of the earth. Production requires very little in terms of raw materials. Certainly no education is required in the conception. The burst of birth brings some pain, but by all accounts, not as bad as a toothache. And voila! Another human being is produced.

Historically, there is a need for people. They would be workers or fighters and in old age insurance. Children were useful in marrying for monetary or military alliances. Nations always promoted birth because the numbers of soldiers and populations always determined temporal power. Churches were interested in the size of congregations as a sign of the truth of their dogmas.

Were any of these reasons for the birth of Yasmin? She may have been born without forethought – culture, convention and hormones could be the answer.

Psychologically, the idea of immortality is innate in the human race. It can certainly be achieved by great feats of courage, conquest, and genius. But how many humans have that in their crystal balls? Perhaps there is always a hope that, well, perhaps greatness is not for me, but all my faults will be eliminated in my progeny.

This little Yasmin will have the same hard road in learning to talk, walk, and make her way in the harsh world. And what is waiting for her? Work, marriage, child rearing, sickness, death.

The gift of life! The joy of life! There are a few moments of existence where reality is suspended and happiness ensues but so many people escape this life in drugs, in alcohol and other addictions, chemical and psychological. Life is painful. Life is boring. Life ends in death. Leda saw her childlessness in terms of the highest selflessness to her unborn children. She saved them from living.

That night she heard a small sound and found that Yasmin had wakened and had crawled to the side of her bed. She leaned over and found the small creature trying to climb into her bed. Leda bent over and pulled Yasmin up and took her in under the covers. She had never slept with a child before and was afraid to leave her there. If she should fall asleep, she could roll over on this tiny body and squish her. Yasmin clung to her with a little shiver. The child smelled warm and sweet, like a cookie. The child's skin was so soft and smooth that Leda caressed her little forearms and said aloud, "This is why people like children." This emotional reason was outside the realm of her rational philosophy. Leda fell asleep with Yasmin in her arms.

"Mama" Yasmin screamed and wakened Leda. She quickly pulled the child to her. She got up and, hugging the little girl, tried to rock her but Yasmin screamed louder. She felt the bottom of the wet makeshift nightdress. She removed the wet cloth and enclosed her in a towel. Leda's head was pounding from the drinking of the previous evening. She could not see taking care of such a needy, squirming, screaming kid; she could not be saddled with Leile's issue. *I must find her family or pay someone to raise this child.*

It was mid-morning when she realized the need to speak to someone about Yasmin. She asked Aliyah to tell her who would know of such matters. Aliyah referred her to Social Services for Refugees. Leda called and the woman who answered had a very heavy French accent. "Genvieve Dorsay, how may I help you?" Leda explained her problem.

"I am sorry but it would be difficult to find the family. I need more information. Where is this girl now?"

"Yasmin is temporarily staying with me at Dr. Aliyah Najjar's home. Madame Dorsay, perhaps we could meet. I really must present this in person."

"I live quite close to Dr. Najjar. I was a patient of Dr. Abdullah Najjar before his untimely death. It would be most convenient for me if you could visit me at home."

She shared a light lunch of tabouleh and lamb with Aliyah. Yasmin had already eaten and was taking a nap. Leda told of her plan to visit Madame Dorsay and asked for permission to use the car and driver. A sudden thought occurred to her, "Aliyah, why don't you take in Yasmin? You have no children, you are alone. You would have a daughter."

"It is impossible for me to even consider such a thing. One cannot substitute a lost child with another and now that Abdullah is gone, I have other plans for my future. My life plan may place me in danger and it would not be a fitting climate for a child." She decided not to ask any questions until Aliyah herself was ready to explain her enigmatic statement.

Madame Dorsay's address was a nearby block apartment building. Leda left the car and approached the entryway devoid of any architectural style or decorations. The small lobby had a rusted panel of apartment numbers but before she could find the right one, the door opened and a small, rotund woman with white hair and bright red lipstick opened the door. "Welcome, Dr. Eimont." Madame Dorsay had an exceptionally warm smile.

Leda followed her up the stairs with peeling paint and graffiti being the predominant features of the dirty hallways. As they entered the third floor apartment, Leda entered another world. Persian carpets of a beautiful luster were a base for the stark European décor with Mies van der Rohe chairs, modern paintings, and a sleek black leather sofa. A heavy glass table rested on what looked like a Henry Moore sculpture. In the corner stood a Giacometti, Leda's favorite artist. She thought of the Giacometti exhibit in Manhattan.

The work was a wood board within an indented track. A ball was placed in the track. There was also a small indentation outside the track meant to hold the ball. It was obvious that the ball must go around the track and never be able to reach its resting-place. How much frustration, disappointment and sadness were conveyed in this most simple wood object. Giacometti was a genius.

"I'm sorry, what were you saying?" Leda apologized for being lost in thought. "I was just admiring your Giacometti."

"Yes," replied Madame Dorsay with a smile, "it is my treasure. Giacometti once said that if a house with Rembrandts and Rubens and a cat were on fire he would save the cats. However, if this place burned, I think the only thing I would save would be this Giacometti."

Leda described her favorite Giacometti.

"Oh yes, 'Circuit, 1931.' I have seen it in Paris," said Madame Dorsay pouring a glass of red wine for Leda.

"I am amazed at this apartment. Did you move it in its entirety from Paris?"

"My personal history is rather bizarre. My husband was the Ambassador at the French Embassy and I did some volunteer work with Palestinian refugees. My children were grown, living in Paris, and I found a great deal of satisfaction in my work. I guess it was just the saint in me evolving. My sainthood was sorely tested when my husband left me for a young, French secretary at his office. We divorced, he married her and now they are back in Paris. I did not want to return there with my defeat obvious to all the people I had known, so I decided to stay. Now, I don't know, I am becoming immune to the suffering so perhaps I am doing less for my psyche, but

I am at the same time more efficient." She told her story in an impersonal way and yet Leda could sense her sadness and resignation. Madame Dorsay offered Leda a cheese tray and another glass of wine and continued, "But enough about me, do tell me how you think I can help you."

Leda again recounted her history with Yasmin. "I really need to find her family so that she can be among her own people. I feel somewhat responsible for her so I would be glad to contribute money on a regular basis for her upbringing. I will pay for her education."

"And if we do not find any family…" Madame Dorsay interjected.

"Then, I would like to know what the fate of these orphans is."

"The fate of these orphans is pathetic—with or without a family. The children of Palestine are now starving and 60% are severely chronically malnourished. There is no schooling for them. They are being systematically exterminated. Why don't you take her?"

After a long moment of silence Leda said, "I'm too old. I don't have the patience. I would have to take her back to the United States, but my conscience would lead me to raise her as a Muslim. You do realize what the situation is for Muslims in the United States right now?"

"Dr. Eimont, do you hear yourself? This is a child who will probably die if you desert her and you are worried about the implications of child-rearing. Give me all the information regarding this family and I will try to do my best to find Yasmin's closest relatives."

Leda pulled a package of papers from her purse and

handed them to Genny. "My whole life has been without children of my own because I didn't want any. To burden myself, at my age, with raising someone else's child—it would be insanity."

"You have a good twenty years to give to this girl. In the United States it will be better than what she is facing here in a refugee camp. I think that God put her in your path. And think of the rewards. You will have someone who will truly remember your life and regret your death."

"Genny, I have thought about this all my life and have never wavered from my earliest conclusions. Child-rearing is not for me." Leda suddenly realized it was after midnight, and after fond farewells, she ran back to the sleeping chauffeur.

Aliyah, drinking coffee, looked up as Leda entered the breakfast area and recounted her visit to Madame Dorsay. After a silent moment Aliyah spoke, "I have known your feelings about children since college but most people, like Madame Dorsay, may find your attitude cold and selfish. Although knowing your reasoning, I understand you."

Yasmin appeared for breakfast in a big pink sweater. "We must go and buy her some clothes. She is a very bright little girl. I've tried to teach her some English."

Yasmin preened and looked up at Leda. "Tank yuu". Leda flushed with pride and love that welled up instinctive, unbeckoned. *I am sinking into bondage, into emotional attachment, and it will just make parting more difficult.*

It was almost two weeks before Genny got back to Leda. "Leda, I have found some of Yasmin's family, but they are in

Gaza. We could go visit if I get permission. I will probably be successful because of my connections with the French Embassy." It took another week of bribes and long waits but finally Genny was able to call and say with glee, "Permission granted!"

CHAPTER 16

The trip with little Yasmin in tow was grueling considering they were held up for twelve hours at the border crossing. Leda saw the horror of Gaza. There had been a recent bombing by Israeli forces: houses razed by Israeli tanks, the lack of any water or sanitary facilities and everywhere Israeli soldiers with submachine guns. Surrounded by miles and miles of walls and barbed wire— the whole place was a concentration camp.

Their driver finally came to a huge ditch cut into the road and apologized as he said he could go no further since the Israelis had closed off the road. They would have to walk the last two miles to the village of Leran. As Leda walked, she noticed little, overweight Genny having a hard time keeping up. However, when they saw the sick, the invalids and children being carried, they realized that it was far easier for them to walk.

"Genny, how can people accept a life with so many difficulties?"

"Perhaps this is the only life they have ever known since the 1967 occupation. That is a whole generation that has only had the experience of being an occupied underclass."

"But they know of a life like ours in the West. They have television, the Internet, so they know other people live in freedom and comfort."

"Yes, it is precisely that knowledge that fuels their rage."

Reaching the village, Genny asked a passing man in Arabic about Yasmin's family and they were directed to a bombed-out building. As they moved the carpet that made a makeshift door they saw six people huddled in the dark. Genny greeted the group in Arabic, introducing herself, Leda and Yasmin. A veiled woman motioned for them to enter and introduced herself to Genny as Fatima. The dirt floor was covered with several piles of rags that served as bedding. One man was moaning in the corner.

"What is wrong with that man?" Leda asked.

Genny translated, "He needs medical attention, but they could get no medical help. He has been bleeding and experiencing difficulty urinating with severe pain."

"He needs a hospital!" Leda said, "He has bladder cancer that is advanced."

"The Israelis do not give permission," was the reply.

Genny then had a conversation with Fatima in Arabic while Leda looked around. She had never seen worse living conditions. Fatima got up and offered Leda and Genny a small plate of olives and two glasses of water. "Fatima is apologizing for the meager repast but wanted you to know that it is no indication of the richness of the welcome they would like to convey." Genny translated in a chocked voice full of emotion. Leda was very touched.

Leda learned that Yasmin had an aunt, a teen-aged girl, Nura. There was no one else. When she was told of the fate of her sister, Nura broke into a deep wailing that was echoed by the whole household. Nura would take Yasmin and reached out to take the little girl. Yasmin clutched Leda desperately screaming "Mama! Mama!" Leda held and rocked Yasmin until she was quiet again; then she gently put Yasmin on the floor beside her.

"Leave her here and let us go," insisted Genny. "This is her family and they will do their best for her. Leave them some money and you can always send additional funds later." Genny started to gather her things as Leda gave Fatima a wad of bills.

Leda, with a heavy heart and a sigh, looked at Yasmin and started getting up to leave. The little girl ran over and clung to her leg with a strength and fierceness she could not believe yelling "tank yuu", "tank yuu". Leda disengaged herself and went through the door, in spite of the shrill scream that Yasmin produced. Leda turned back and picked up Yasmin. *I could no more leave Yasmin than I could leave my arm or leg behind. This child is mine.*

The three of them made the two-mile walk back to the checkpoint. They had to stop frequently for tired Genny whose blisters forced her to walk barefoot. Leda carried the tired child and found her arms aching with fatigue. They did not bring food or supplies and Yasmin started to cry adding to the difficulty of the journey. *What have I done? This was an irreversible decision. Now Yasmin is mine.*

The turmoil of her thoughts was heavier than the weight of Yasmin.

People on the road looked in amazement at these two western women walking with them. They finally stopped to rest and an old man seeing them explained to Genny in Arabic. "There was a suicide bombing in Tel Aviv, so the soldiers at the checkpoint are especially difficult." The old man also offered them some water and some figs.

The line at the checkpoint lasted into the evening. Mortified that she had to go to the bathroom out in the open, Leda found some cover behind a scraggly bush. The sun had set and it was getting very cold. Yasmin was shivering. Leda took off her white wool shawl that she had tied around her waist and wrapped Yasmin in it. Three hours later, they finally were in front of the checkpoint. Exhausted, Leda placed sleeping Yasmin, completely wrapped in the shawl, by her feet.

Out of the corner of her eye she saw an Israeli soldier approaching. He was carrying a rifle and as he held up the rifle he looked at the bundle at Leda's feet. He raised the rifle, pointed the barrel at the white bundle and thrust. Leda jumped back and screamed with horror. The bundle moved and the white wool became soaked in red. The soldier, in a state of shock, jumped back. "Oh no!" Leda fell to her knees opening the bundle. Yasmin was spurting blood from a huge gash in her neck. Trying to stop the bleeding by pressing the shawl into the wound, Leda screamed, "Get an ambulance!"

The crowd surrounded the scene but made no moves to do anything. Genny ran up to the soldiers at the checkpoint and demanded some help. The soldiers said that they would do their best to get an ambulance and started shouting orders. Leda saw the Israeli soldier who had stabbed at the bundle, a boy no older than 18, with horror on his face and tears in his eyes, come up and say, "So, so, sorry. It was an accident, it was an accident. I thought maybe some weapons or contraband. I was just trying to open the bundle."

Leda almost fainted - the blood, Yasmin's faint gurgling, the spurts of blood coming from the arterial wound. Leda was on her knees compressing the right side of Yasmin's neck with force. Yasmin's eyes were wide open with terror and held their pleading gaze at Leda.

"Please God, let Yasmin live!" Leda screamed up to the sky.

Leda knew that at home in the States with emergency help being minutes away there would have been a chance to stop the bleeding, to operate and suture the cut carotid. Here in Gaza on this dusty desert road all she had was a blood-soaked shawl and her fingers. It was hopeless. "Yasmin, hang on, hang on." whispered Leda through her tears as she saw Yasmin's eyes become cloudy and the spurting of the blood ceasing. To die of exsanguination was to have life flow out stealthily, quietly. The blood now oozing made Leda aware of how much blood covered them both and how much had seeped into the land of Gaza.

She knew Yasmin was dying. Leda picked up the little body from the ground and tried to keep it warm by hugging it close to her heart. Genny reached over and closed Yasmin's eyes. Leda did not move for an eternity while her mind raced. *Why Yasmin? Why now? What evil in this world led to*

checkpoints? To fear and hatred so extreme? I know part of me
also died on this dirty, blood-soaked spot in Gaza. Yasmin was
an accidental love that ended in accidental death.

Finally, after two hours, an ambulance arrived. The
soldiers shouted at the driver for the delay. The driver
staggered over to the bloody tableaux and said, "You see, she's
dead – there's no need to rush." The soldiers, realizing they
were dealing with an American citizen started apologizing
and offered to drive them back to Damascus in their jeep.
Genny called Aliyah and told her what had happened. Genny
tried to take Yasmin's body away from Leda but she held on
for the entire five-hour journey. Leda, covered in blood and
still refusing to release Yasmin was met at the door by Aliyah
who gasped at the sight.

"Leda, get a hold of yourself. It was an accident."

Leda got a bath and a tranquilizer after a long tussle with
Aliyah to forcibly release Yasmin's body. The day passed in
tears of grief. She moved around the house with a vacant stare
not comprehending what had occurred or why.

The Muslim burial ceremony was new for Leda. Aliyah
took the blood-spattered body and, with some women, washed
it three times and wrapped it in a white shroud. The next day
they had a Muslim funeral at a mosque in Damascus where an
Imam intoned: "All who are on this earth must die according
to the Quran." The tall Palestinian continued, "Remember
the destroyer of pleasures, death, for not a day passes upon the
grave except it says 'I am the house of remoteness, the house
of loneliness. I am the house of soil; I am the house of worms.'"

The small gathered group chanted over and over, "La
ilaha ella Allah." Leda knew this was "There is no God but

Allah." She herself said these words over and over again as she also prayed to the Virgin Mary and Christ and all the saints for a better place for Yasmin than this world.

Only men were allowed at the burial, so Leda knew she was seeing the small, white shrouded body for the last time. She wanted to wail and loudly moan with the rest of the women to release all the agony of grief. But the heavy sedatives and the warning from Aliyah that only the ignorant wail and moan at funerals kept her silent.

Later, crying in the stillness of her room her thoughts were booming a thousand decibels. Her abhorrence of all injustice and suffering produced a symphony of hatred so horrific that she had to put her hands to her ears to drown out the piercing, painful sounds. The injustice of it all! A knock on the door from Aliyah made her run to the mirror to try to apply some powder to her puffy eyes and red nose. "Leda, you have a visitor, Dr. Talib al-Zawahiri is here to express his condolences." Leda put on her dark sunglasses and went downstairs.

Talib came up to her and the touch of his hand upon hers was electric. She looked up at him as he, with undue familiarity, took off her dark glasses. "You have been crying." Leda felt some anger at this exposure and started to object and take back the dark glasses. However, all the events of the past months surrounded her: Arthur's death, the misery of the clinics, the horror of the West Bank, the hell of Gaza, and now the murder of innocent Yasmin. She felt new tears running down her cheeks. Talib took her in his arms and she sobbed even louder at this unexpected embrace. Inhaling his aroma of eucalyptus she felt a desire to stay in a cocoon with him to the exclusion of the entire world. She needed protection against the darkness. Leda explained that now she truly understood the reality of the Palestinians. Talib was silent but she was aware of the beating of his heart.

Aliyah stepped into the room and her look drove Leda into a more proper pose. Talib turned to Aliyah, "Yasmin was fortunate to leave this world and all of you are crying. An Arab poet once said that when you are born you are crying and all the people around you are happy, but when you die you are happy and the people around you are crying." Talib turned to Leda. She saw the outline of a gun under his jacket as the sun struck the back of his suit.

"For a Palestinian to die these days it is a blessing. Life holds no promise," Aliyah said very quietly as she scrutinized Talib and Leda. She knew that some understanding had passed between them and she became afraid for her American friend. With a sigh, Aliyah said, "Leda, perhaps you should go back to the States. In your current emotional state, it would be very hard for you to continue your work here. After a good long rest, you can always come back."

Talib looked at Aliyah in surprise but then added, "Yes, I agree, it would be best for you to go home. But before you go, perhaps you would consider a trip to the desert with me."

Angry, Aliyah said, "Talib, No! What could you possibly be thinking?"

Annoyed, he looked at Aliyah and said, "It would be remarkable medicine for Leda who has experienced the sickness of Middle East injustice."

Confused about Aliyah's reaction Leda felt that her present, pervasive, numbness might be cured by the desert.

She recalled all her desert dreams. *All I have to do is to show some courage, some disregard for the strictures that have bound my life and find release. To go with Talib would be most unconventional but I am beyond caring. I have been robbed of all I loved in life. This may be my last opportunity to experience the joy of life.*

"Yes Talib, I would love a trip into the desert."

CHAPTER 17

Aliyah gave her some djellabas and abas, quite a few bottles of sun block, and some kid boots. "It gets very cold in the desert at night" she said as she put some warm sweaters in Leda's pack. "Travel will be by horse and camel with seven servants to help and you will have a tent pitched every night." In spite of her helpfulness, Leda sensed that Aliyah condemned this trip. She saw how Aliyah followed Talib suspiciously with her eyes. Leda put on her kaffiyeh and looked at herself in the mirror. She tied a silk scarf around her loose, blue djellaba and was pleased. When she put on her scarf to hide her mouth and nose, only her eyes shone with relief and mystery.

The next morning Aliyah drove Leda and a servant to the starting point of their journey. Abla was a pudgy, young Palestinian who wore the white and black Palestinian kaffiyeh. Aliyah spent the ride giving rapid directions to Abla in Arabic and apologized for not being able to find an English-speaking servant for Leda. They arrived at the outskirts of a slum area where a small herd of camels gathered. Talib seemed pleased upon seeing her in her Arabic garb and had sharp words with Aliyah in Arabic.

"Our trip will take us about one hundred miles east of Damascus to a place called Palmyra; the camels can make the trip in about 3 to 4 days. There are places along the way to rest but I will take a route through the desert so that you will know how the Bedouins live," said Talib with a smile. "You will experience our ancient way of life."

Leda had read *The Sheltering Sky* by Bowles about the great romance of the desert. *Was it really that romantic with no modern facilities in the tent? What about going to the bathroom, taking a shower, putting on my cosmetics? But I want to dispense with my whole circumscribed, orderly life so I must completely ignore all my doubts, hesitation. I will just absorb life. Many humans manage to survive this way, I will too.*

Standing in the sun waiting for his camel to be packed, Talib spoke about the history of their trip, "Palmyra is an oasis in the middle of the Syrian desert, an ideal stopping place for caravans trading in silk from China to the Mediterranean. Rome conquered Syria and the oasis became known as a city of palm trees, or Palmyra."

Leda absorbed these facts. "So it started as a Roman colony?"

Talib, moving them both into the shade, continued, "Yes, the Romans treated its people very well. Persia and Rome were at war and the ruler of Palmyra, Auzaina, was able to defeat the Persian Army."

"I read that it was called the Rome of the East at its height."

"Yes. But Auzaina was assassinated in mysterious circumstances and his second wife, Zenobia, a strong woman, took power."

"I've heard of her," said Leda as she inspected Tala, her camel. The wind was whipping up some sand so Leda covered her face with her scarf.

"Queen Zenobia, an accomplished, intelligent woman, claimed to be a descendant of Cleopatra. She spoke many languages, led her own army, and managed in five years to create a wealthy and educated empire. Greek philosophers taught there and the architecture was so outstanding that the ruins are admired by tourists even today." Talib helped her up on her camel and gave some answers to the servant Karim regarding the order of the camels. He returned with a lit cigarette.

"What happened to Queen Zenobia?" Leda asked in a lilting tone of flirtatiousness.

"As always," continued Talib, "there is lust for more once the appetites are aroused". He looked into Leda's eyes with such intensity that she was forced to look away. "Queen Zenobia's ambition to get rid of Roman domination grew to a desire to conquer all of Rome. The Emperor Aurelian was engaged in many conflicts at the time and this enabled Queen Zenobia to take over all of Syria, Egypt and Asia Minor. She took the title of August, which was only used by the emperor of Rome, and had money struck in her likeness. The Roman emperor, fearful of Zenobia's increasing power, destroyed the city and massacred its people. Zenobia was brought back to Rome in gold chains where she poisoned herself."

"Is this a warning against ambitious women?" Leda asked with a smile.

After the poor areas of the outskirts, the full emptiness of the desert with its undulating, changing landscape appeared - the sand in ribbons of gold against the blue sky. Leda was floating in a sea of shimmering waves of sand. The air, dry and fresh smelled of the perfume of nothingness: purity, simplicity, and starkness—the desert Leda had dreamed about. Leda became aware of her burning hands. As she removed her sunglasses she saw that they were a bright pink since she had forgotten to apply sunscreen. After four hours, her back started to ache and she was very thirsty. She took the flask hanging by her side and drank greedily. She also needed to urinate. Talib was riding in front of her, in silence, and she did not want to request a stop.

After another hour, Leda experienced acute discomfort, and, to her relief, Talib finally gave the signal to halt. Abla lowered her camel, stepped off, went a few steps, spread out her robes for modesty and squatted. As she got up she pushed sand over her effluent like a cat. Yes, this was just like a big sandbox. Leda followed suit, jumping off her camel. Abla helped her spread out her cloak as Leda squatted in the desert sand.

She noticed Talib observing this with a smirk. He turned away, just as Haldoon and Mohammed did, and sent streams into the sand. Leda accidentally glimpsed Talib's penis and felt a rush, a physical reaction and flushed in shame. Her heart was pounding and she could not get the vision out of her mind. *I felt I had died with my mother, with Arthur, with Yasmin, how can it be that I am experiencing such a primitive desire?*

Relieved, they had cool tea from a jug and Abla served lamb and cucumber sandwiches. Soon they remounted and it was not until the sun started its descent that Leda, forgetting her pain, observed the sunset, a spectacular palate of purple, blue and red. In seeing this supreme visual beauty Leda understood she had seen the apex of God's handiwork on this earth.

They stopped their caravan and Haldoon and Mohammed helped Talib put up two tents with unbelievable slowness. In the meantime, Abla was unpacking carpets, pots and pillows so that in an hour they had their home in the sand. Leda inspected her cushioned area for sleep and lay down stretching her back. After the heat of the day she felt the rapidly cooling air. Shivering with cold, she was looking for the sweaters that Aliyah had given her, and she felt Talib's body embracing her from behind. "It gets very cold at night. It's almost as if the sand turns to snow in the moonlight." Talib turned her around and looked into her eyes. She looked back and realized what the term Islam meant. It meant submission. She felt as if her soul had left her and placed itself at Talib's feet.

Abla came and broke the spell, indicating that dinner was ready.

They ate in a circle around the fire and the aroma of the lamb and vegetables permeated the whole tent and warmed them. Leda ate with gusto but felt left out of the conversation in Arabic between the men. Since Abla spoke no English, Leda had time to observe in silence. Haldoon was a Bedouin, an extremely handsome man with classic features, dark skin and brilliant green eyes. Mohammed was a dark skinned, brown-eyed Syrian who seemed a match for the roly-poly Abla. She noticed that Abla looked at Mohammed with distinct longing. Leda only longed for aspirin and rest.

With morning came a breakfast of goat cheese, olives, tea and bread. Leda felt a surge of energy and excitement. *I feel alive again. Is it the desert, or is it Talib?* The day passed without awkwardness because the rules had been established. In the evening they set camp near a small town.

"This is a stopping point for tours to Palmyra. After dinner the servants are going to have some fun with the tourists. Do you want to go, Leda?" *The last thing on my list of desires is to mingle with tourists.*

"No, Talib, this is my only chance in the desert and I would prefer to stay here. I am sure I would be quite safe here, so you go ahead." *I know I will not be left alone.*

They sat in the tent by candlelight. The flame was playing with the interwoven colors of the carpets and the designs of the pillows. Abla had left them hot tea and very sweet dried fruit. *For the first time I don't care how I look. But I have to get my mind going to get rid of this sinking feeling in the pit of my stomach, this vacuum of desire. Leda, be true to yourself, my thinking has always controlled my feelings.* She was aware of Talib staring at her intently and she plunged into conversation.

"Syria is alone in the Middle East by being self-sufficient in terms of food or energy. The main problem is that due to sanctions they are having a hard time getting replacements for their airplanes and cars. Flying is rather unsafe because of this in Syria. They could buy them from Russia which with Iran…"

Talib, surprised by her lecture, interrupted. "Leda, be sincere with me. Is it not you and me that you would really like to discuss?"

Leda was shocked at his frankness. "There can't be a discussion of this sort. I would never intrude on the relationship between you and Aliyah."

"A relationship! What can you possibly mean by that?" Talib asked with sincere surprise.

"Why, every time you speak with me, she seems so angry and I assume it is some type of jealousy. But my friendship with Aliyah means more to me than a flirtation with you." As Leda said this, she lowered her eyes.

"Aliyah is angry, but not because of a romantic jealousy. She's angry because she thinks I'll be trying to seduce you to my cause. She is concerned about your safety." Talib lit another cigarette.

What cause?" Leda asked with a trembling voice. She felt a deep sense of disappointment and shame at her presumption that this handsome young man would have a physical interest in her.

"You are familiar with the Palestinian situation—the greatest injustice of modern times because it is perpetrated by a civilized society on the stage of a world which pretends blindness." Talib stood up as if he were going to give a lecture but he saw how tired and sad Leda looked, as if all her vitality had crumbled. He put his hand on her shoulder, lifted her chin, and looking into her eyes said, " Perhaps we can discuss this another time."

Another long day in the sun passed approaching Palmyra on the swaying camels. Leda felt as if she were sailing on the sand drifting into the unknown future. *My ideal, enviable life has an empty center, a void. I want to love, to soar, and to feel truly alive. I want to blot out pain, suffering and death no matter what the consequences.*

CHAPTER 18

Arriving at Palmyra, as Leda dismounted from her camel she dropped her passport. Before she could retrieve it Talib picked it up and looked through it. "Not a flattering photograph. But citizen of USA is a wonderful appellation." As Talib flipped a few more pages she snatched the passport from him.

"Would my being American have anything to do with your concern for me? Aliyah has warned me about you."

"Leda my cause is for the liberation of the Israeli Occupied Territories which is criminal under international law. I am privy to a secret plan to cripple the occupiers and to free my people. This is what Aliyah is fearful about. She thinks I want to involve you."

"And do you? Want to involve me?" Leda was incredulous. "What could I possibly do for this cause?"

"I want you because you are so familiar with the Palestinian situation and you are brave and intelligent. I feel you are the woman I have been looking for a long time. I will make you aware of where my soul is soon."

Palmyra at sunset was a magnificence of glistening golden ruins, splendors of ancient architecture, and echoes of lost civilizations. Leda gasped at the sight. They laid camp with an early night in mind and Leda used a flashlight to study her guidebook. The visit to the ruins would cover an area of six square kilometers.

Since the servants had seen Palmyra and would not understand Talib's English explanations, Leda set out alone with Talib. With a wealth of facts and anecdotes he showed her the Baal Temple, the Arch of Triumph, the Baths, the Straight Street, the Congress Council and the Cemeteries. With a backdrop of sunset and pink and ivory ruins they climbed a steep hill overlooking the remains of an Arab castle, the Qala'at ibn Maan.

They sat down on a large rock. "Talib, you are so mysterious. We really must be open with each other. We must not play games. I am ready now, please tell me everything."

"About my attraction to you?" Talib asked, looking into her eyes. Leda became confused and sought to escape a revelation of her own feelings.

"No, tell me about your cause and what role Aliyah has in it." As she said this, it became clear there were more people involved as she remembered the mysterious meetings with people in the middle of the night in Damascus.

"Leda, this is dangerous knowledge. It involves the exposure of an Israeli plot. My brother obtained this plan in Egypt and he had it translated from the coded form. It was written by an obscure Egyptian rabbi but it is called *Zion's Plan for the New Millennium*."

"Oh no!" cried Leda with distain. "Talib, don't tell me that you are reviving the discredited Protocols of the Elders of Zion! Anti-Semites have used that for years to establish that there is a Jewish plot to gain world control. I read it in college when it was fashionable to read 'forbidden books' such as *Mein Kampf* and the *Kama Sutra*."

"You must understand," continued Leda with passion, "I respect the Jewish religion as I do all religions and understand the unfairness of anti-Semitism or any type of racism. I am not against the Jewish people but against Israeli State endorsed Zionism! For example, I hate Communism but have never had any rancor against the Russian people, or as much as I hate the idea of Nazism, I do not feel hatred for the German people. It seems Israeli State policy cannot be criticized without the emotional turmoil of accusations of anti-Semitism. Now the Protocols are anti-Semitic because they are not against Israeli policy, but against the Jewish people."

"Tell me, what do you remember of this book?" Talib asked with great seriousness

"Well, the book surfaced during the Russian Revolution and Henry Ford published it in a Detroit newspaper. It dealt with Jewish control of much of the world's money and the world press. They exercise power through the Kabbalah which are esoteric teachings meant for the higher initiates of the Talmud. They always believed the Messiah would be a temporal king who would make Israel master of the world. I remember being shocked reading that the orthodox Jew is not bound by principles of morality towards people of other nations. It was funny that it spoke to how Jews should make their sons lawyers and doctors since this is the dream of every

Jewish mother in the United States." Leda was laughing but she noticed Talib's serious expression and tried to remember what else was in the little book. "I vaguely remember, as a Republican, being amused at the book's statement that liberalism will help them in their cause, as well as big government. That is all I can remember except that the goal was the establishment of a Jewish state in Palestine."

Talib was playing with a stick in his hands and at this point snapped it. He looked up at Leda and said, "Yes, you remember quite a bit. As you know, much of this is true. Chiam Weitzmann and others worked desperately to get the Jewish people a homeland. Weitzmann succeeded in getting the Balfour Declaration passed and Israel became a State in 1947. However, these days Israel is not a safe place due to the Palestinians who want their land back."

As they started walking Talib continued. "A plan was devised by a rabbi, Levin, in Egypt to crush the Palestinians' desire for justice. The whole world is in sympathy with the Jews due to the Holocaust and Levin wanted to exploit it. He laid down the means to increase the power and safety of the Jewish state by promoting Israel through lobbying and control of the media. Any promotion of Palestinians would be considered anti-Semitic. Arabs would be associated only with terrorism and the destruction of Israel. Multiple wars in the Middle East would antagonize the Arabs and keep the American military present for the defense of Israel. Since Israel would be the only friendly power in the Middle East, it would demand expanded borders and expulsion of all Palestinians from their lands."

Talib threw down his stick and with a voice hoarse with

emotion said, "So you see, Leda, there is no hope for the suffering Palestinian people. They are going to be crushed by this bulldozer in motion."

Leda came up to Talib and said softly, "What you say is not so secret since most of it is coming true. Why all the secrecy?"

"My secret is my desperate attempt to reverse the course of things"

"But what can you do?" Leda asked as she felt Talib's arms around her body. Leda could scarcely breathe. She was aware of a soft warm wind caressing her face and the aroma of eucalyptus. In the distance the sunset turned all the ancient rocks into luminescent jewels. She felt suspended in time and space.

"Leda, my group wants to put a dagger into the heart of injustice by beheading the monster. Will you help?"

She tried to answer when Talib took her in his arms and kissed her. His rough beard was scratching her sunburned face and his tongue was wet in her mouth. She could not think because her body responded mindlessly. She felt Talib exploring her through her folds of fabric and found herself wet with anticipation. He did not enter her although she knew he was more than ready. With a yell he let go of her and turned away. *The yell is a means of self-control, a waking from blind desire.*

"Let's go Leda, it is dark now and I am feeling darkness in my heart and mind." He took her by the hand and they went back to camp. Leda entered her tent touching her face and ran to a mirror to confirm her reddened face. She was astounded by the physical reaction of her body longing for

Talib. Flashes of desire and frustration shot through her body like viral invaders. Years of marriage had settled sex into an activity instead of violent passion. Approaches from attractive men were welcomed flirtatiously but rebuffed. Her standards excluded casual sex.

Now my body is in full submission without reservation. As she threw some cold water on her face, reason took over. *But this is not for me, this ridiculous passion with a young man. I must edit my life and expel these feelings. An affair with Talib? Impossible. At my age I am losing people - Arthur's death completely set me adrift. I see myself as a balloon tied down to reality and with each death one more string is cut that had tethered me to life. With all strings cut I am floating, released from confinement. But released to what? If I am on the verge of loss of self, what difference does it make? But it would negate my principles, my whole order of things.*

Abla had a hot supper waiting and Leda went to sit in their semi-circle. Abla smiled when she saw her but immediately lowered her eyes.

CHAPTER 19

Leda and Talib finished their breakfast alone as the servants prepared the animals to leave. Leda rose to return to her tent and Talib reached over and grazed her nipple with his fingertip. The nipple stiffened through the gauzy material. Leda felt as if she had lost all self-control. "No!" she hissed at Talib. "You must not do this to me. You're playing with me."

"Yes, I am playing, and it is fine play! This embrace is written about in the *Kama Sutra*. It is called the piercing embrace when a woman is bent over and the man touches her nipples. Do you not study the art of love?"

"I've not had the time or the inclination to delve into mating activity studies in my life. It seemed to me to be more germane to know about the world and why I am here than to know about reproducing," Leda said with a loud sigh of justification.

Talib grimaced, "There is more to the *Kama Sutra* than mating. It describes the ancient Hindu view of life. There is

Dharma or virtue, Artha or wealth and Kama or pleasure. All three are necessary to human life. It seems to me that you have wrapped yourself into Dharma and Artha all your life without ever having experienced Kama."

"I am surprised that as a Muslim you would take this Hindu gibberish seriously. If you are looking for an alternate philosophy, you should consider Buddhism. The Lord Buddha advises a renunciation of all pleasure since earthly desire is the cause of all unhappiness."

Talib turned to go but hesitated. "You are the strangest woman I have ever known. You try to do everything to make yourself attractive, yet repel advances. You are a conformist beyond belief and yet you are childless. What is a woman without a child? You do not lack the nurturing feelings or you would not have loved Yasmin or been so devastated by her death. Why the enigma?"

Leda looked up at Talib in anger. The sun was in her eyes and she saw in shadow only his white eyes and his brilliant white teeth. "What is a woman without a child? A complete person! Is there a dearth of humanity? And what is the quality of most of them? It is the lowest quality that reproduces most. As a man you only have to spray your seed while a woman has to carry the perfect parasite in her body for nine months. I believe the most precious quality of life is freedom and once a child is born, that child is a responsibility forever. If you think you can make me believe that a child is necessary, you are mistaken."

Talib listened to this diatribe and softly asked, "What about Yasmin?" Leda's eyes filled with tears and she knew she had no answer. She left abruptly to calm herself.

A long journey home in the shifting sands and high winds gave Leda a sense of physical discomfort to echo her emotional turmoil. *Could my whole life been lived under the wrong set of rules? Did I construct a universe based on the wrong premises? And now obviously, it was too late - much too late for love, or children, or a life more attuned to the pleasures of the body. No! I did know love. I loved Arthur with all my heart. But it was the love of continual habit—love of familiarity, comfort, home.*

My attraction to Talib is a love of the imagination, and I had felt this often with various men. My imaginary love affairs gave me love without the venereal diseases, unwanted pregnancies, angry wives, divorce complications, stepchildren, financial entanglements, betrayals, and sad endings. I also had variety of lovers and situations not present or available in real life. Certainly these scenarios were outside of reality, but how pleasant all these fantasies were. But they did not provide all - especially what I felt when Talib grazed my nipple.

Their caravan stopped for lunch and as they finished, the sky turned dark. Talib and Mohammed looked at each other with dismay. "It is a sirocco—a high wind. We will not be able to continue. Leda, come to my tent and the servants will add reinforcements to insulate it further. They are not as afraid as you will be once it starts." Talib took Leda and they settled on the carpet as the wind started to shake the tent that the servants had just managed to put up. The sides of the tent were being crushed and she felt as if she were on a boat caught in a storm. She could actually see fear on Talib's face as he bundled her up, told her to lay low and went out to check on the camels. As the opening moved to let Talib out,

Leda felt the full force of a spray of sand on her exposed face. She quickly covered her face with a scarf and curled up to minimize her body. Talib and Mohammed yelled instructions and prepared for the siege.

The roaring and the ripping of the wind shook the small tent. At last Talib returned and found Leda shivering. He lay down next to her and she found herself pressing against him. Talib started to explore her with his hands. Leda said "No!" very harshly. "I do not want to be made a fool of Talib. I have not lost my mind. What am I to you but a relief for your bodily needs? You can have Abla or any of the other servants for that. You do not need me."

Talib looked at her with surprise, "Leda, I had no idea you thought so little of yourself. I find you extremely interesting and attractive. You are not just a sexual object to me but a personification of my deepest desires. I had never expected to have such depth of feelings, emotionally as well as physically for such a perfect woman."

"Perfect?!" Leda broke out laughing.

"There, you are beautiful when you laugh and let yourself go. Don't be so proud of the strength of your discipline; rather be ashamed of the weakness of your passions."

Leda looked at him and all her deliberations fell apart. Talib wet his finger and outlined Leda's mouth in a slow, circling motion. She felt her lips swelling and her mouth fill with saliva. All the while he was looking directly at her eyes until her eyes fell to her own heaving breasts. Talib held her breasts and she felt her nipples stiffen and a warm sensation begin in the pit of her stomach. Talib held her in silence for so long that she was beginning to feel anxious. He then exposed her breasts and, sitting across from her very gently started to push his nails in a semi-circle around each nipple in turn. Talib reached over and got a mirror and said, "Look how beautiful, Leda."

Leda was mesmerized by their appearance, the stiffness of the red, erect nipples and the swollen aspect of her breasts that she had never seen before. She became excited looking at herself. He then leaned over and suckled each in turn, at the same time flicking his tongue and gently biting. His hands started to move downward and for a moment Leda stiffened. As she felt the length of his body by her side she knew what pleasure must be contained in the appendage that was stiff with blood. She pushed him with a force born of a terror of violation, but Talib had the upper hand. Their bodies blended in the frenzy of anticipation and excitement. Leda's hunger was as acute as her anger and there was nothing responding except the primitive brain cells reacting to the sensations that Talib knew how to evoke. And finally she did not think.

The storm, whirling and thrashing outside, mirrored their lovemaking. It was half terror and pain as well as the most acute feelings of pleasure and union. She felt parched after her long denial of bodily needs and, now in the quenching, she feared she would drown. At last they were sated.

They fell asleep entwined and when they woke it was dark and quiet. The storm had passed. *This is my first exposure to this narcotic. Would I ever be able to stop?* As she pondered her dishevelment and her awareness for the need of a bath and food she started to feel Talib's hands calling to her again. All other needs were forgotten in a repeat of unbridled lust.

After a brief rest Talib went out and brought her some

fruit and cheese and as she ate Talib asked, "Do you value your life?

"This experience was so essential even if it would cause death I would not have done without it. Talib, I would have died without having truly lived if this had never happened."

Talib turned away as he said, "Leda, death is a very high price."

CHAPTER 20

Returning from the desert Leda did not want to see Talib again for fear of reality seeping in. She wanted memory to gift-wrap her experience so she could take it out in private and not have it exposed and ridiculed by the world. Talib aroused an addiction and her body, in exquisite torture, yearned for him constantly.

Knowing that this obsession was hopeless and would never have an imprint on reality, Leda tried to guess the meaning of this attraction and pondered numerous hours playing solitaire. *Is this true love? No. Is this a way of showing me God's Will? No. Is it punishment for the carefree life I have mostly led? No. Is it so I would fall in love with life so deeply that when I die I would regret the loss of life? Yes.*

Aliyah guessed at what happened during their trip and seemed full of contempt for Talib. "Why do you disapprove so much?" What is the danger that you see?" asked Leda.

"I love you like a sister but you must understand that Talib is not just an innocent suitor for your hand. In the first place he is married with a wife and four children. He also has a mistress and a daughter living in Egypt. His sexual prowess is well known in Damascus," Leda was astounded by these revelations, but refused to let it intrude on her reverie. She smiled.

Aliyah in disgust continued, "He is not a secret diamond in the rough. You have been blinded by a superbly cut and brilliant stone that is known to all. He uses his sexual powers to aid his aims and obtained many state secrets by his seductions of diplomat's wives. Talib is brilliant at lovemaking and seduction but the only thing he really loves is his political goals. He is a genius and a fanatic. And he is ruthless in his use of people, especially women, in order to achieve his aims."

Leda took Aliyah's blunt truth without any visible distress. She knew that Talib was not promising her romantic love or even affection and there was no future for them. She just wanted enough of a hold over him so that he would not stop these sensations. "What are his aims, Aliyah? What would he want from me?"

"I'm so sorry to talk like this. I have known you for so many years and I know that you have completely lost yourself in this man. I warned you—not to prohibit your happiness, but to protect you."

"Aliyah! You must tell me. Now!"

"Talib is the ringleader of a group of terrorists centered in Egypt. He has plans for activities in the United States. When I told him of your presence in Damascus, his curiosity was about your reputation and social standing in the United States. He was especially impressed by your wealth and your political connections. Leda, now that I have told you, and you see the danger, surely you will avoid him."

How can I avoid him when I feel the giddy, incomprehensible joy of love? I know this is the wrong person and an inappropriate time and place. I never sympathized with weakness of body or mind but these cosmic lessons now make me understand human weakness, addiction, and loss of control. Against all rationality the image of Talib was imprinted upon her brain every waking moment.

Leda did not see Talib for a week and since her visa was expiring made plans to return to the United States. She received an invitation to the French Embassy for a reception and Talib would certainly be there. As Leda took a bath and put on her silky underwear, she had images of what Talib would do to her body and felt the spasms of happiness start to flow from her inner being. The orange silk dress shot with gold brocade—that would express her desire. She looked at herself in the mirror and noticed her flushed complexion and sparkling eyes. "Yes, orgasms are a great beauty boost."

The Embassy's grand reception room was overflowing with people and Leda was immediately surrounded by a group of Americans. She talked about her work and her trip to Palmyra while drinking a Martini. From the corner of her eye she saw Talib and a beautiful young woman. She was a classic, Middle Eastern beauty with a Grecian profile and long, silky, black hair that glistened in the candlelight. She had a superb figure in her modest black sheath, which, nevertheless, revealed more than it concealed. Her most remarkable trait was her carriage that was proud and statuesque. Leda suddenly felt old and unattractive and ridiculous as she saw Talib and the woman approaching her.

"Leda, I would like to introduce you to my wife, Myriam," Talib said with a smile.

"I have heard much about you, Dr. Eimont. I hope that Talib treated you as a proper guide on your trip to Palmyra."

"Yes, he was the perfect guide. Excuse me."

Leda, stunned by this bizarre incident, went to the rest room where she observed her white face in the mirror. *Did he tell his wife about us? Did they share a joke? Perhaps Myriam would never suspect her husband of sexual activity with this old American woman.* She was looking for a way to exit the reception when she came face to face with the French Ambassador. "The reception is lovely but I am afraid I have a headache and must leave." After calling Aliyah's chauffeur, Leda waited outside for the car to arrive.

Talib pulled up in his small Mercedes and said, "Leda. Get in." He got out of the driver's side, opened the door, pushed her into the car, and accelerated out of the Embassy driveway. He drove in silence for a long time up into the hills of Damascus. Then he stopped by a house in the middle of an olive orchard. "Come, Leda, I will show you the house I grew up in." Leda followed him into the deserted house. As soon as the door was shut, she turned and hit his face with all her might.

He was stunned and shouted, "Stop, Leda!"

"You bastard, why did you humiliate me? I knew you had a woman. I am not naïve, but you know I'm leaving. Why parade her in front of me?"

As she moved to strike again, Talib restrained her and

pushed her on an ancient sofa. "Do you want me to make love to you?"

Leda looked at him in disbelief before she heard herself saying in a husky voice she did not recognize "Yes. Yes, Talib. Please, now Talib."

"Then seduce me, Leda, make me want you."

She found herself unbuttoning her orange silk dress as the shame and humiliation of her position burned her face. Talib coldly observed and said, "Enough. You disgust me with these actions. Do you not understand that when a man is seduced, he is only seduced through the mystery of his own imagination? Acting like a cheap whore is not seductive." Leda felt his words like a slap in the face. Becoming even more furious, she picked up a silver candlestick and was about to strike him with the intent to kill.

"You do have the passion to kill," Talib said as he grabbed her. She bit his wrist until it drew blood. Talib made love to her as if it were a death struggle. When they had no more energy Talib looked at her and said, "Now you have had it all. I have no more to give. Anger is the best aphrodisiac and I wanted you to experience the intensity of anger combined with lovemaking. It is well described in the *Kama Sutra*."

"Was all this only a lesson in sex? What is it you really want from me?"

Talib looked at her and said, "I want you to join my movement in America. I had to know you physically in order to ask. I had to make sure that you were not just an intellectual in terms of causes. Intellectuals think too much for action. But in lovemaking I am able to determine your physical passions and courage. I think you have both." Leda was trying to process these past few weeks in terms of an examination. *Had she rated an "A" for effort?* Leda heard with clarity the next sentence from Talib: "I know how you feel about the American-Israeli policy toward the Palestinian people. I know you want to help, but how much are you willing to sacrifice?"

Leda was taken aback by these comments. She had very strong feelings about the injustice in the Middle East, but to face danger, to betray her country? No wonder Aliyah did not want her to be near Talib. "You want to take my life the same way you took my body?" she asked in disbelief. "There is no way I would consider such a proposition."

She straightened her clothes and started to leave when Talib stopped her. "You are a woman who has had everything and has had nothing. You are a woman who desires to show the world that she has lived. You were created for the grand gesture, the impossible sacrifice, the historical event. You were not meant to go home to a round of teas and charity work and good books. You were meant to burn yourself out in passionate lovemaking and to go up in the flames of martyrdom for a just cause." Talib was looking so deeply into her eyes that she felt hypnotized by a laser beam.

For a long time there was absolute silence. *True dramatic dialogue is the art of omission.* "Think, Leda, think! Death at the hands of history is the only death which contains the seeds of life."

"There is no way I could be a terrorist." she said vehemently looking away.

"Leda, you will. And you will say, 'Yes, Talib, please, Talib,' and 'now Talib.' You will welcome the martyrdom of Islam with the same fervor that you welcomed my body. There is a theory that the greatest orgasm is felt in death." He took her confidently in his arms as she acquiesced. They went out into the cool night air and drove to Aliyah's house. She was glad all were asleep to hide her bruises and torn clothing.

Sleep would not come as Leda tried to process the full flavor of Talib's request. *He wants me to be a martyr, to die, and perhaps kill other people. And he has considered others, like Aliyah, for his plot. I am not an exclusive woman in his life, and yet he has seduced me. He is always in my thoughts, my body longs for him. I cannot resist him. What is love if it is not unconditional?*

Leda knew she would not be returning and tried to finish her clinic patients. *To be a political martyr was ridiculous. The drama of a swift death is appealing but I have a terror of hurting other people.* Aliyah gave her books on Islam and Leda became increasingly immersed in the simplicity and beauty of the religion. It revolved around only five principles. The first was Faith, "There is no god but God." The second was prayers said five times a day, the third was Charity, the fourth was Ramadan, the month-long fast, and the fifth was a pilgrimage to Mecca. Leda considered Islam to be the newest and most modern of the world's religions.

One night Talib came for a meeting and the men left at midnight. As Talib was the last to leave she followed him out into the garden where and he turned toward her and embraced her. The air was fragrant with rosemary and the moon was full. "Our future is written in the stars. You know the inevitable," he whispered to her gently. "I am sorry in a way to have intruded on your life. I truly love you, Leda. You may not fully comprehend what this means but I would be ready to die for you. I think about you every day and question whether I should ask you for a sacrifice as great."

"I am leaving for home in three days," she whispered as if it were a secret. "What is your plan?"

"I can only tell you that the details will emerge as you make a commitment that you will take part. There can never be direct communication between us. It would be too dangerous to the cause." Seeing her sad eyes, he continued, "I could never leave my people. I just want some justice. Will you be my vehicle of justice, my avenging angel?"

"I have made no decisions. Who would suspect Dr. Leda Eimont to be a terrorist?" Leda said with a bitter laugh.

CHAPTER 21

Coming home from the Middle East, Leda needed familiarity, rest, and friends. She arranged to have Sophia and Leslie meet her at a luxurious spa in Sedona. Perhaps she would be able to process her turmoil reflected by the opinions of her friends.

Leda felt the blast of a hundred degree day in Phoenix and appreciated the cool air of the limousine at the airport. The two-hour ride north to Sedona exposed beautiful red rocks jutting into the vast aquamarine sky. Entering the gates of the private resort, passing breathtaking grounds, she registered and entered their reserved cottage. The seven rooms contained Indian artifacts, Western Art, and oversized earth tone furniture on natural stone floors. Leda perused all the literature promising enhanced beauty: nutritious zero calorie foods; classes to strengthen, elongate, and tone the body; hikes through the acres of grounds.

Unpacking in the sunlit room, she took out her magnifying mirror and saw flesh hanging from her facial bones. *The signs of irreversible decay.* Stripping to shower, she saw the uneven skin tone of her body. *Exercise and cosmetics will not postpone the inevitable. How could I let Talib make love to me, … I could not let him see this old woman… his request to give my life for a greater cause…. a martyr? … the deceit at Gainer… an evil government … I am destined to stop this evil … destroyed by eliminating its head… the head of the United States government… How could I kill a high government official protected by stringent government security…? my life sacrificed for this cause? … Would I be a terrorist - a freedom fighter? … would it lead to justice? …. Or would I just be lumped into another one of the "crazies"?*

America based on fairness… helping all the peoples of the earth… I loved the decent America of my youth… Was it all a lie even then? … Was there just as much deceit, and corruption… was I too blind to see it? … Why do I care so much? … Was I even considering this outlandish idea to please Talib? I will never see him again… He has all these other women… Why had he chosen me to be his avenging angel? He promised me immortality….I want to protest … I want to show the world that I lived… Was this why Talib sought me out?

Leda had already received her first instruction from Talib through Aliyah, "Find a way to ingratiate yourself with the highest levels of Republican causes. I am sure that you know high government officials that could introduce you to White House events." This message aroused Leda's curiosity and challenged her ingenuity. *I can do this, I will raise my political profile, and then, when the rest of the story is revealed to me, if it is so terrible I cannot take part, I can just opt out by saying I have changed my mind.*

The next day, Leslie arrived eager to hear the whole

story from Leda about the Middle East. Her eyes opened in disbelief as she heard all the details of Leda's passion for Talib and her tragedy with Yasmin. Leslie sighed and poured Pellegrino into both of their glasses. After a sip she said, "How are you, Leda. I mean, really?"

"I'm disappointed in life. Apparently the world is full of pain and injustice but we live by the grace of a happy blindness. Perhaps awareness grows out of our souls in hours of pain and panic and we see the world in darkness as it truly is." Leda stood up and looked down sadly.

"I have envied you all my life. You must be depressed to make such statements. But that is understandable considering what you went through with Arthur and Yasmin." said Leslie with real concern.

"I'm confused, but I know that I am destined to do something," said Leda with an enigmatic smile. I must do something for the Palestinian people."

"But are you not forgetting the problems of the Jewish people? asked Leslie.

"There are over 2 billion Christians in the world, 1.5 billion Muslims and a little less than a billion Hindus. How many Jews are there?" queried Leda. "The answer is 16 million worldwide but their influence is enormous."

"Enough about religion and politics! When Sophia arrives, we must be very kind because, as you know, Conrad is having an affair. She needs our sympathy and advice," Leslie said as she reached for more water.

The next day the door flung open to a gypsy apparition. Sophia had arrived. "Why the delay?" questioned Leda.

"Romance on the plane from Boston with a handsome

journalist. If the layover would have been any longer I would have had a real lay." Sophia said with a laugh.

Leda hugged her, "Sophia, you are positively glowing. We must hear all about your escapade! By the way, there is a delivery for you." An enormous bouquet of long-stemmed red roses stood on the table. Sophia opened up the note.

> *Sophia, my only love, forgive my insanity.*
> *Debbie and I are through and I only want you*
> *for the rest of our days. Love, Conrad*

Sophia's heart leaped at this peak of good fortune. The man on the plane was a thrilling boost and now Conrad crawling back.

"All right ladies, time for drinks. Our last chance before they put us on their spa starvation diet and run us ragged with exercise." Leda announced.

Sophia returning from unpacking in her room exclaimed in a shocked voice, "Leda, you're smoking!" as she saw Leda light a cigarette.

Leda, sitting on a sofa, blew out a stream of smoke and said, "Nicotine is not so bad. It does help to prevent weight gain and is supposed to prevent neurofibrillary tangles. When I can't smoke, I use a nicotine patch." Leda made light of one of the main worries of her life. The idea of the tangles of Alzheimer's resonated with Sophia knowing Leda's history with her mother's Alzheimer disease.

Leda, with a Martini held court, "…so I decided to give a fund-raiser for the Republican Party. Their convention will be in New York next year and I decided to make myself useful.

You must help me plan what would be a most spectacular event that could attract the Vice-President's wife. I was thinking of a Fourth of July party."

"You're not thinking of poisoning the punch, are you?" giggled Leslie knowing of Leda's new zeal against the government.

"Poisoned punch would not be Leda's choice," remarked Sophia. "She would more likely spray the crowd with an Uzi."

"Ladies, ladies, enough kidding around," Leda cut off the conversation. "Perhaps I could influence Middle East Policies with this administration."

"So what are our complaints at this advanced age?" Sophia ventured.

Leda said, "I will tell you a Russian fairy tale: An orphan was taken by her evil uncle to die in the forest so he could have her wealth. The cold wind blew and the snow fell but she did not complain. Finally ice started to form all around her and still no complaints. The god of winter saw all this, withdrew, and put her in a bubble of warmth. Some peasants came by and she told of being an orphan and being left in the forest. They attacked her uncle; she got all her wealth, and lived happily ever after. The moral of the story is never complain."

Only you, Leda!" said Sophia with a shaking head, "answering with a Russian propaganda tale."

Sophia, basking in front of the flowers, launched into a detailed description of her recent adventure in Los Angeles to gales of laughter.

Leda monopolized dinner with her plans for her

fundraising. "It will be a Fourth of July lunch for hundreds. Republican Women for President Brown. I will invite Amy Chester to be our guest speaker."

"Do you think she will come?" asked Leslie

"For $50,000, it is a sure bet she will come. After all, I am serious about making a name for myself with this administration."

"Then, I will hold a small, black tie dinner at home for a fee of $25, 000," continued Leda, "and invite 24 couples who are social climbers and would be delighted to attend an intimate dinner with Vice President and Mrs. Chester."

"Vice President Chester, how do you know he will come?" doubted Sophia.

"Elementary, my dear. Once I get Mrs. Chester to realize I can raise money, the wife will have the last word on her husband's decisions."

Sophia was calculating that for a guaranteed million dollars she was sure the Chesters would show. But why was Leda in such desperate straits for the Conservative Party? She was so violently against the policies of Brown in the Middle East. Did she really think she could change them?

In the morning, Leslie led them on a five-mile hike through the mountains followed by classes in Pilates and Yoga. The afternoon was devoted to facials and manicures. During the Spartan evening meal Leslie talked about her doubts about the validity of polling. Sophia, after her third glass of wine spilled the whole sordid story of Conrad's affair. "Debbie is pregnant and Conrad suggested an abortion but I would take Conrad back on the condition that we adopt the baby"

Leda was appalled, "Sophia, you are doing this just for revenge." But she understood the rage of revenge is very sweet.

Returning from Arizona, Leda had an appointment for a physical. It had been originally scheduled before the trip to the Middle East but she had no need of all these unnecessary tests. She called the office to cancel her appointment but in a split second she decided to go.

Her physician, Dr. George Levy—thin, tall and rumpled—had been a year behind her at school and the most brilliant person in his class. His practice on Park Avenue was closed to new patients, but Leda always had first priority. In medical school, he used to follow her around like a puppy, full of admiration and longing. Her tests were done last week and now the consultation.

"So, what is the verdict, Georgie? Am I going to live?" Leda could not resist flirting with him because he always turned such a beautiful shade of red.

Dr. Levy, taken aback, did not react in his normal fashion. "Leda," he began, "I have bad news for you. Your brain scan showed some abnormal changes and, with your family history and blood tests, I cannot rule out the possibility of early Alzheimer's disease. There are some medications these days that can delay the onset of the disease if we catch it in its earliest stages." Leda was thunderstruck. The news could not have been more horrific- the one thing in life she dreaded above all—the slow disintegration of her mind. She quickly thanked Georgie and escaped home.

I always had contingency plans based on various scenarios. I must be in control and it must be now before the disease starts to steal me from myself. I will not suffer and be a victim. I will take my own life! There is an organization in Switzerland Dignitas that helps people with assisted suicide. Yes, to fly there, have a prescription for barbiturates, and then drink my way to eternity while being filmed for legal reasons. I want dignity, not degeneracy into a mindless flesh. But if I am to have a rapid exit, why not make it meaningful, make a statement of my deepest beliefs?

CHAPTER 22

Events must revolve around a centerpiece, whether it be the bride, the corpse, or, in this case, a celebrity. Leda turned the ivory card over several times before calling Mrs. Chester's private number, "Dr. Leda Eimont," and was put through immediately. Leda launched into a little recap of their meeting at the Conservative Club. "Mrs. Chester, I am planning a fundraiser, a woman's lunch here in my home in Greenwich. I was wondering…"

"My schedule is very busy Dr. Eimont. I would love to be your guest, but…"

Here, Leda interrupted. "Mrs. Chester, I am not asking you to come as a guest. I am asking you to be our luncheon speaker for a fee of $50,000." Leda knew this was double her usual compensation. "And Mrs. Chester, your talk could center on your book and we could have a book-signing after," Leda said soothingly. There was no preparation necessary and especially no worries about answering any political questions. Just one wrong word sometimes made embarrassing headlines.

"Why yes, I just might make time for this occasion. What are the possible dates?"

A date in July was possible and Leda held out for the fourth. This presented some difficulty because her husband, the Vice-President, was committed in Washington with the President, but the prospect of the fee let her declare her own independence for the day.

Dawn on July 4th was sunny, clear, and in the upper 70s. Leda chose a white dress and a navy blazer. The theme of red, white and blue was apparent in the tents on her laws waiting for the two hundred guests. Putting on her gold jewelry she thought of Arthur. *He would definitely think it an extravagance—with the fifty thousand-lecture fee and the forty thousand cost of the lunch it is ninety thousand of my money. But the price is immaterial. It is a step in the completion of my goal.*

The black limousine whisked Mrs. Chester in at 11:30 surrounded by two secret service men and an assistant that was introduced as Lorrie Mesa. Leda greeted them warmly and led the two women into the guest suite for Mrs. Chester to freshen up. Lorrie had a small suitcase that held some cosmetics and a change of clothing that was identical to what Mrs. Chester was wearing. "I always buy several of the same outfit so that if there are wrinkles or a spot, I can change without appearing to have changed clothes," Amy confided to Leda.

Tuxedoed male waiters holding trays of Champagne, Bloody Mary's, and Perrier greeted the guests. Women in black and white were passing trays with caviar and sour cream in baby potatoes, shrimp wrapped in coriander leaves, baby lamb chops, smoked salmon rolled with cream cheese, and miniature Peking duck packages. Leda observed some of her richest friends gobbling this food as if they were starving. At the other end of the spectrum there were the size zero ladies with lusting eyes, examining and imagining, who refused all enticements while sipping their Perrier.

The lunch at 1:00 served an appetizer of crab cakes with guacamole sauce followed by filet mignon or striped bass. The meal ended with a salad followed by a variety of cheeses and fruit. Mrs. Chester gave her speech about her book that was humorous and completely generic -she said nothing and implied nothing. *Here we are in a world with so many horrors and injustice, and the wife of the second most powerful person in the America acts as if she were asleep.* The audience gave her a standing ovation.

The speech was followed by coffee and a variety of miniature cakes and cookies. Mrs. Chester, eager to get back to Washington, thanked Leda for the exceptional occasion. Leda gave her a small box of pastries "for your trip back, since you are missing dessert," Mrs. Chester smiled up to her from the limousine window and said, "Leda, I think we are to be very good friends."

In the following months, Leda ran into the Vice-President's wife on several occasions. She joined her causes and contributed generously. She gave Mrs. Chester medical advice and scheduled a priority appointment for her in New York. She approached Mrs. Chester with the possibility of an intimate party in her home for about 40 people and asked if she would come with the Vice-President. Leda saw the imposition and hesitation on Amy Chester's face.

"I can only speak for myself. You see, I don't control Dick's schedule," answered Amy.

"I understand. I just think that at $25,000 per person… I can guarantee 48 people and the Conservative Party could certainly use a million dollars. As a matter of fact, I will guarantee a million if you and Dick show up." Even though President Brown's campaign coffers were full, Leda could see that the Chesters would be responsible for a substantial contribution.

"I will speak with Dick. I will try my best."

A week later Amy called and gave Leda two possible dates. Leda started calling in favors and found the act of begging unusual and demeaning. The dinner took three consultants, the chef of the best restaurant in Manhattan and a million dollars of Leda's funds requiring the sale of some stocks.

The evening, planned with cocktails on the terrace and then a formal dinner, displayed the best of the Lodge household. As she surveyed the six tables of eight strategically placed throughout the rooms the silver gleamed on white cloths with candles and flowers arranged in an autumn motif. Leda herself dressed with care. *She must appear elegant but not ostentatious—she should not upstage any of her guests. She must play the role of powerful yet humble servant of the Conservative Party.*

Leda had asked the Chesters to stay overnight, but they demurred due to security reasons. They would be leaving immediately after the main course by helicopter to Washington. Leda was glad of her large lawn and was intrigued by all the security precautions.

"This is a dangerous time, Mrs. Lodge," said Jack Austin of the CIA after introducing himself. "There is a reason we are checking your water and your garage. Now I know, ma'am that you have the highest security clearance, being a friend of Mrs. Chester and all, but you can see our responsibility."

"Of course," Leda agreed, "you never can tell where enemies lurk," Leda said with a straight face. "These are dangerous, frightening times."

"Yes, ma'am. There are all sorts of ingenious ways that the terrorists have come up with. But thanks to Homeland Security we are a step ahead of them all the way."

Sophia was the first to arrive in a black velvet dress that enhanced her voluptuous figure and she had her dark hair piled high in a style of a Grecian princess. Conrad, as always, was morose but Leda could sense his excitement at being close to the centers of power.

Leslie arrived next in a black tuxedo and somehow this overtly masculine look made Leslie look feminine since she had always looked uncomfortable and awkward in dresses. "Leda, I have to talk to you about Gainer. I had no idea that anything unusual was going on there. It only started to look suspicious in the face of your insistence on government conspiracies. Now I know that the polls are skewed to reflect the interests of certain parties. But what can I do? This is too big of a conspiracy for me to take on. I don't think anyone would believe me. Do you remember how we laughed at the 'vast right-wing conspiracy' that Hillary Clinton uncovered? Would it not be better if we both laughed off this one?"

Leda looked at Leslie with a startled expression, as if her dearest confidant had suddenly lost her mind. "Leslie, you are letting the aura of the power of the United States of America get to you. You love this country, and so do I. People working for their own interests and the interest of a foreign government have kidnapped this country. We must expose these lies. I am willing to die for this country if I could save it."

"I have been in the corporate world long enough not to want to be a whistle-blower or a malcontent troublemaker. I have seen how these people end up – outside the mainstream. And the corporations go on. I do not want to sacrifice everything to be in the right. That is not my fight."

Leda rushed off to greet some more guests and Leslie felt that Leda was in a manic mood of dangerous proportions. She had energy, influence, intelligence, and money. Her talk was getting more radical but it was probably due to Arthur's death. She would hardly be one to throw her energies into a sewing circle or a country club. No, Leda chose political action and looking around her, Leslie concluded that Leda certainly succeeded.

The helicopter was settling on the lawn. The twenty-five thousand dollars gave the guests a photograph: an entrée into fame. These photographs, a most exclusive decoration, would be silver-framed and casually referred to, "Yes that is us with the Vice-President and Mrs. Chester. We were invited to dinner with them."

Dinner was an unqualified success. The Menu cards, inspired by a Durrell novel, read:

Oysters Rockefeller
Montrachet
Double Beef Consommé
Amontillado
Broiled Lobster a la Marechel
Dilled Cucumbers. Potatoes a la Duchesse
Filet Mignon a la Rossini
Chateau Lafite and Rinnart Brut
Fonds d'Artichaut Farcis
Pommery Sec
Sorbet au Kirsch
Cheeses: Pont l'Eveque; Rocquefort.
Coffee
Madeira

For Leda, money was power: the key to influence, to social success and status. Perhaps it was not possible to buy love, but it was certainly possible to buy friendship. This was confirmed at the end of the evening when liquors and chocolates were served and the Chesters were about to leave. Amy Chester took the check for one million dollars from Leda and thanked her "very good friend" for her efforts toward the Republican Party.

The helicopter lifted away with wind and fury and everyone returned for coffee - a truly successful evening. Leslie caught up with Leda on the lawn. "Leda, how extraordinary this event has been. You suspect the government of evil behavior and yet you can stage a gigantic, expensive love-fest for these very people. How do you justify this?"

Leda smiled, "Why Leslie, I thoroughly considered all

my options and the most effective way to changing policy is from within."

Leda stripped off her dark green gown revealing her silky orange bra and panties. She had always gained confidence by knowing she was superbly dressed and her underwear gave her inner confidence. The dichotomy brought her thoughts of subterfuge and secrecy. *It is amazing how our interior and exterior could be so at odds without anyone being the wiser. Talib would be pleased with my success.*

She sank into the tub pouring in bath salts called "Jasmine." Leda recalled the dark eyes and the helpless clinging limbs of the little girl who had died so brutally. Her numerous complaints to the United States Embassy were rewarded with a steely silence. The Israelis could not stop apologizing and said this tragedy forced them to issue new directives to the border guards. *A Palestinian life had no more worth to them than that of a mosquito.*

Leda started to cry and her tears were flowing as she pulled the stopper on the bathtub. The water whirling in concentric circles down the drain mesmerized her. She had once considered why the water did not just go straight down but learned that the whirlpool was the result of adding motion to the water in the tub during bathing. The motion had to go somewhere. It won't just disappear because nothing ever disappears. Just like my emotions and convictions, she thought, they do not disappear; they form my own kind of whirlpool.

CHAPTER 23

Leda arrived in Florida where she had a vacation home in the exclusive gated community of Vista Lago. The cool, large spaces were defined by the views of the ocean and the white and blue décor. She opened the sliding doors and inhaled the salt air. The water was so blue and the sky so bright that it provided some relief from her political obsession.

Mail included an invitation to a cocktail party at the clubhouse. She would have lunch, then a long walk on the beach and a swim in the ocean. She phoned the Vista Lago restaurant and ordered a cold lobster salad. She turned on Wagner's *Tristan and Isolda*, and the building of tension without culmination was genius. She listened to John Adams, her favorite composer, as she ate her dinner. But neither the food nor the music captured her attention.

Leda as a major Party fundraiser found frequent invitations to Washington circles. The conferences and think tanks regarding the direction of the nation's policies were just a diversion because policy had been set. The question of the Middle East was much discussed. The underlying truth was that oil, profits of private military contractors, and the protection of Israel were the basis for US policy. Everyone understood but had no more freedom to say it than the peasants who were supposed to observe the King who had no clothes.

Walking along the ocean, Leda's thoughts had the background sound of crashing waves. *To act or not to act? Either way it would end in death.*

With the whole world on the list of dissension, the United States still insists that it is right in its policies. The plight of the Palestinians is hopeless and there is no room for an objective view of the Palestinian "terrorists." Even the terms are nonsense. Is defense of one's home a "terrorist" activity? What is the difference between a patriot, a resistance fighter, a freedom fighter and a terrorist? Were American Revolutionary forces terrorists? Were French fighters against the Nazis resistance fighters or terrorists? The definitions are coined according to the prevailing interests.

The winners write history.

Since its creation Israel has received 1.2 trillion dollars in forms of direct aid, loan guarantees, and military grants. For all this money, has Israel offered any meaningful benefit to the United States? In what war has Israel fought alongside the United States? Exactly what strategic interest of the United States does Israel serve? Is there anyone left in the Middle East that Israel has not antagonized? Israel's garrison mentality, long record of occupation and violation of international law was matched with its artificial creation by colonialists. The interests of the Palestinian people were completely ignored.

The fat cats in Texas sitting by their computers punching

out numbers to deploy "smart bombs"—could they be considered heroes by any human standard? Now there are very few medals for bravery because it is so hard to determine who punched the bomb button and how brave it was. They were safe in their war rooms backed up by billions of dollars of technology. Compare this to a youth strapping up with explosives knowing that death waits or the Palestinian boys protecting their homes by throwing rocks being mowed down by machine guns and tanks

When she entered the ocean it was already late and she was the only one on the beach. The beach was deserted and a swim would revive her. After a few laps she stood up to leave when a tremendously powerful undertow dragged at her and forced her under. She panicked at how helpless she was and remembered that the key was not to struggle but to let the wave take you out and try to get to shore on the next incoming wave.

To submit... in order to save myself... perhaps it was a lesson... regarding... Talib... key to my destiny... is submission... not struggle.... If I drowned right now... it would be a swift end... wasted death... mean nothing. The incoming wave brought her close to shore, but she had to struggle and was tossed and battered and bruised by the sand. Somehow she finally crawled out of the water. Walking back along the shore she felt euphoric having been so close to danger and death. Danger as an aphrodisiac was a concept that she now understood.

Returning from the beach, she needed relief from her thoughts. *I must go out and see people.* She remembered the invitation on her desk and called her friend Mary to find out more about the cocktail party. Mary and Tim had been among the guests who had come to her fundraising dinner. Mary was a bubbly blond who was a joy to be with because of her supernatural happiness in everything. Mary complimented Leda on her dinner for the Chesters but added, "It's too bad that you had no companion. Has there been no one after Arthur? There is a new man here, recently divorced. I would like to introduce you." Leda felt ashamed as if she no longer had the credentials for a social life.

The party the next evening was held in the Club Restaurant. Healthy, silver-haired people in bright colors enlivened the scene. The drinks were flowing and the conversations getting louder by the minute. Mary greeted her with a warm hug.

Tim launched into a loud discussion, "Leda, I really enjoyed your fundraiser. What a hoot to be able to run into Dick Chester again, after almost 50 years. You know we went to prep school together. He was such a go-getter even as a kid. It makes you proud to be an American. He told me what a tough job he had with all those terrorists. We just should nuke Iraq and Afghanistan, don't you?" A small circle surrounded them and she saw that they were all nodding in assent.

Tim, brushing back his white hair, took another long sip of his bourbon and continued, "I'm sure proud to know that Brown and Chester have the guts to send out our troops and kick some ass. We have a big fight on our hands with all those Muslims throughout the world aching to kill us. Leda, you are a gem for all the work you are doing to support this Party since we have to be strong to go to the Middle East and defend our way of life. It is better to fight them over there than have to fight them here."

Mary entered the conversation with a tall balding man and stooped posture introducing him as Steve Malin. "I wanted you to meet because you both have suffered recent losses. Leda lost her husband Arthur and Steve's son was killed in Iraq." This was to be her initiation into dating again.

Leda shook his hand and expressed her condolences. "He was killed in combat?"

"Well, no. Officially, he was in some skirmish and died from having one of our tanks run into his jeep, but it was because of those desert bastards that he was over there. They should export every one of those rag-head Arabs from here. There is no sense in harboring scum in our own land." Steve said with conviction taking another sip of his drink. "I know you were in the Middle East and Mary even told me there was a kid you liked and wanted to bring home."

Tim realized that "nuking" all those people may not be a solution that Leda wanted to hear. "But those desert bastards killed Steve's son. I can't see you having any feelings for the fucking Arab terrorists." An uncomfortable silence followed as Leda tried to think where she could escape. Tim, seeing her look around, said, "Well, I'm glad that you are working so hard for the Republicans. I know you feel as we do about this country. I'll leave you two youngsters alone."

She would be stuck with Steve for a while. She asked for another drink. There would be no purpose to argue with these people. They lived on a different planet and she could not explain or convince them of her viewpoint. Steve came back with drinks. She tried to find a neutral topic of conversation. "Have you seen any interesting movies lately?" This was as bland as she could stomach. Steve went into a description of all the movies he had seen lately. Leda's eyes glazed over as she made her way out after thanking Mary and Tim.

♦

The time spent in Florida among the aging, conservative, patriotic, rich made Leda feel like an alien from another planet. After five days, her patience had reached its limits and Leda told Mary she had the next flight home. She was very displaced, as if she no longer belonged in the life she had lived.

The first class compartment was empty and she tried to think of the patterns and meanings of events. She must know some truths before her death. *What about my faith?* The dogmas had lost some profundity in the face of her last two years. She collided with reality and her Catholicism offered no direction. Without her faith she faced an even darker chasm of utter chaos without even the simple explanation of the Baltimore Catechism, "I was created to love and serve My Lord and God."

The flight attendant brought her lunch. Leda ate ravenously. Even the dry turkey was delicious as her body demanded food. *Did thinking take up many calories? Compared to walking, sewing, rowing, and running? Is the reason television watching is such a factor in obesity not because of the snacking and the lack of movement but because of the resting brain cells?*

Leda started to read one of her favorite books, *August 1914* by Solzhenitsyn about World War I and the thousands that died every day. *Does the scarcity of deaths in this present conflict make every one of those lives more precious? Are lives of equal value? Equal under God, equal in freedom, equal in justice, and, according to Communism, equal in distribution of wealth. The seven billion are as unequal as the variety of species. The brief day of the butterfly against the hundred- year tortoise; the intelligent fox against the stupid turkey; the predatory tiger against the gentle rabbit. Is it all just the survival of the fittest? If this is so, there is no need for the concept of justice because justice assumes equality. Even in America, the land of justice, this is obvious to anyone that studies the population of 2 million prisoners. How many millionaires are sitting on Death Row? A rich country mourns one of its soldiers in headlines when thousands dying in Africa get a sentence on page four.*

Is justice the sheltering myth that protects us from reality?

Home was a welcome sight and, she went to the kitchen, where she found a small mountain of mail. She put all bills aside and was coming to the end when she saw a letter with a French stamp. Her hand trembled as she opened it.

My Dearest Leda,

> *Our conversations in the desert have bloomed due to the tears of our people. I know you have already accomplished the groundwork in furthering your political reputation. I too have been occupied with bringing our plan to life. We now know that President Brown is to meet with the Prime Minister of Israel in New York in November. Your next task is to be present at this event. At this meeting they are to sign an understanding that there is to be a Greater Israel since the Palestinians as a people do not*

really exist. This must be prevented. The fate of an entire nation rests on our success.

It would be dangerous to meet with you in person, but Aliyah will meet you in Paris. She knows all and we were able to overcome her protestations at involving you by convincing her of the greater good. Stay at the Ritz and she will be in touch on August 8. This will give us a month before the Republican Convention in New York. I send you my humble regards and affection and the blessings of Allah.

Talib al-Zawahiri

CHAPTER 24

One month for decision and preparation. *Was Talib crazy enough to think I could accomplish this? Getting close enough to the President of the United States and the Prime Minister of Israel to inflict bodily harm? How can I make a decision when I don't know the plan, my role in it, or the consequences?* There are myriad ways in which this could be accomplished but after hundreds of scenarios I can't find one that is feasible.

Should I forget the entire proposition? I am a woman of honor, so I know this is the time of decision. I know that I will asked to sacrifice, perhaps to help without participating, but it is quite clear that the danger will involve bodily harm. How can I be a terrorist for a cause without terror? And if the plot fails, and I survive, the public scorn and humiliation would be worse than death. Better a swift end rather than imprisonment, torture. To be known as a traitor to my own country. Arthur... Arthur...

My life, what is it worth? How can I face the loss of my mind, my independence, to be fed, bathed, and diapered? There is Dignitas in Switzerland willing to help me with a wonderful cocktail destined for eternal sleep, the Eternity Martini.

She considered herself a Catholic. Did the faith of 2000 years have any guidance for her? She believed with the primitive instinct of a turtle hatching and groping blindly toward the ocean. An explanation for life was in order. Even after her sophisticated and thorough study of history and religions, she knew she could have no other faith than Catholicism. If she were a Muslim contemplating this act, there would be no soul searching since by participating in Holy Jihad she would be assured of the blessings of Allah and an entrance to Paradise. But she was a Roman Catholic. She would be condemned forever.

What would I be, a Joan of Arc or a murderer? I will be asked to be in a plot to kill, to maim, and to destroy. I could not hurt the smallest living thing and now I am considering killing the President of the United States and the Prime Minister of Israel. Will there be more people harmed? So what is the answer?

She discounted Father Delos because he would object immediately. She needed wiser spiritual guidance. There was only one person that could give her the answer—Father Joseph Picta. She needed spiritual guidance and the ears of a good friend who could keep a sacred secret.

Father Picta, a priest imprisoned by the Nazis for his faith at Auschwitz, had a holy and wise worldview and he would know the answer. Father had had back surgery a year ago and the doctor accidentally severed his spinal cord and Father was left permanently paralyzed from the chest down. "My malpractice insurance will take care of you," the devastated doctor said.

"You were not drunk when you operated; you had no ill will, why would I sue you and damage your record and reputation?" was Father Picta's reply.

Leda knew the physician, a confirmed atheist. She also knew that a friendship transpired between the priest and the physician and that the doctor converted to Catholicism. "You see, Leda, God works in ways unknown to man," Father Picta had said with a smile.

The driveway to the nursing home was embellished with Rhododendrons. The nuns maintained a light and cheerful building; in contrast to the horrors of wasted flesh within. What terror to be among these living dead: the crippled bodies, the vacant expressions, and the aroma of decay. She did not want her life to end in this warehouse of terminal dreams. Leda followed Sister Agnes to a private room at the end of the hall. She had brought liquor-filled chocolates for Father Picta. She knew he was not allowed alcohol and this was a way of having him enjoy at least a memory of the taste. Leda was shocked by his appearance. The once vigorous, strong, handsome man was now a pale, weak shadow.

He smiled as she entered. "Leda, it has been months— only some postcards from Damascus. Have you forgotten your old friend?" His voice was as strong as ever and she bent over to kiss him on his forehead.

"How are you doing Father?"

"Not too bad, Leda," said Father Picta as he tried with a frown to pull himself more upright. "I have gotten over the humiliation of being incontinent but still suffer when Sister Agnes has to wipe me after a bowel movement. God has a way of making a cosmic joke. In Auschwitz there was hunger and torture, but I had not lost control. Now even that is lost, but I offer my suffering for the poor souls who do not even have a clue as to why they are suffering." Father Picta was opening the foil on one of the candies and taking a bite with an expression of pure joy. "To have a reason for suffering is a great gift," he continued.

"And what is your reason for suffering Father?"

"It is in fulfillment of God's wishes, my prayers and sacrifices on the altar of the Lord in expiation for my sins. It is submission to the Will of God. It is entwining of my suffering with the sufferings of humanity and, therefore, entering into a communion of souls longing for heaven—a place free of pain."

"Father what are these sins that you want God to forgive? What did you do that requires such suffering?"

"Not all sins are the sins of action. Sometimes they are the most innocent ones, committed in the heat of the moment due to human failings and weaknesses. But there are others that are worse."

"I don't understand," Leda said with a movement forward in her chair.

"For example, my thoughts are often on my misery, not due to my physical condition but because most of the people here are in various stages of dementia. I have no one to talk with, to discuss philosophy or politics with. The nuns are too busy and their expertise is not intellectual. I miss the human interchange of thoughts—it is a great gift to exchange ideas, to feed the mind. The conversations we had at Auschwitz! I am sure that was the reason why some of us survived. Here I am bereft of that and guilty of the worst—hubris. Yes, Leda, pride. Pride in my intellect and pride in my superiority over these demented fellow souls. Pride is the sin that led to the fall of the angels, the worst sin of all. It was a worse sin than the disobedience of Eve that only led to exile from Paradise. But pride led the fallen angels to be demons—the birth of evil."

Sister Agnes interrupted the moment when she brought in tea and delicious cookies baked by the nuns. "Could we bring you lunch, Dr. Eimont?

"No, thank you, Sister. These cookies are wonderful and much appreciated."

There was silence as Leda noticed several patients being wheeled outside. *How could Father Picta think it was a sin to think he was superior? He was a genius who spoke five languages, had three doctorates and had written dozens of books.*

"Leda, you know how I would love to discuss the world situation with you, but I could tell by the sound of your voice when you said you would visit me that something is on your mind. What is it, my dear?"

No one since Arthur could read her so clearly. She told him the story of Damascus, Yasmin, the Palestinian camp, Talib, and now her final commitment to the cause. Where did she stand? What should she do? She expected Father Picta to stop her. The end never justifies the means and there would be violence involved, she was sure. Father Picta was listening with his eyes closed. When Leda looked at him she thought he was asleep. She stopped talking and he opened his eyes.

"Your intentions are good. You want to help people who are unjustly treated. I did the same for the Jews in Germany. I once saved a Jewish boy being carried away by a Nazi by hitting the officer in the head with a rock and then grabbing the boy and hiding him. I never knew if I killed him, but I never considered that action immoral or a sin. So how can I judge you? If I were in a position to save thousands of Jewish people by a heroic act of violence such as wiping out Hitler and the German High Command I might have done it. God has given you a choice far harder than any I ever faced because the ethnic cleansing of the Palestinians is not as overt as the Nazi plague, but I believe that there is truth on your side. There will be killing involved but it falls under the laws of war, though undeclared, and as our government calls it, an asymmetrical war of a nation with the most modern weapons against stones and suicide bombers," continued Father Picta.

Father Picta closed his eyes and then said softly, "You must pray and God will give you the answer. I will offer my sufferings for the next month so that you make the right decision." Sister Agnes entered and said that it was time for Father's physical therapy.

Driving home, Leda was praying but no answer came. No booming voice from God. How difficult it is to fulfill God's wishes when there are no signposts, no maps, just an amorphous sea of possibilities. She would revert to chance for her decision.

She pulled into her driveway. Leda made a Martini, sat down on the white sofa, and took out the deck of cards. She could not stand indecision: a wrong decision is better than no decision. She played cards. Black meant NO and red meant YES. A decision left to fate: a Jack of Hearts. YES. *The door opens and I step into my future.*

CHAPTER 25

Arrival in Paris brought a sense of coming home since she spent much time here with Arthur walking the boulevards, studying the art, and eating the delicious food. Every corner brought memories. The elegance of the women had decreased, but fashions change. The Ritz was the quintessential Parisian Hotel on the Place Vendome. Madame Lodge received a heartfelt welcome to her suite done in soft tones of luxury and good taste. She had brought an enormous wardrobe to be dressed for the occasion for her last stay in Paris.

The decision made, she knew the time of her death—September, during the Conservative Convention in New York. It simplified things. No more wondering what diseases were wired into her genes, no horror at an impending helpless state in some nursing home, no worry about her worldly wealth. All these problems fell away except the fear of pain and the unknown.

The call came on the appointed day, in the morning, after breakfast. "Leda?"

"Aliyah! How wonderful to hear your voice."

" Meet me at Café Alexandria, in the Arab sector at noon."

Leda dressed with care and applied her scent of Jasmine, which enveloped her in that unconditional, innocent love. The black, formfitting suit was flattering and she decided to put on her red hat. *Just in case Talib would show up.*

The Arab sector of Paris was large and exuded all the flavor of the Middle East. The beautifully flowing inscriptions of Arabic were upon all establishments. Women were veiled and men sat at the sidewalk cafes in animated conversation. The cab driver stopped at a small establishment that seemed closed. All the chairs were still set on the tables outside.

"Quel est le tarif?" Leda asked before peeling out a generous amount in Euros as she left the cab. She looked at her Cartier watch surrounded by diamonds. She was early and a young man came out and started to set the chairs at the outdoor tables. As she sat down, the restaurant door opened and Aliyah came out. She looked the epitome of the elegant Parisianne in a beautifully cut, grey checked suit.

"Leda! I was waiting inside. Come!" Aliyah kissed Leda warmly. "Let us have champagne to celebrate our reunion. This once I feel I will have a sip also." Aliyah said as she picked a window table in the deserted restaurant. "It is too warm outside."

A waiter came by and Aliyah ordered champagne and a variety of Middle Eastern foods. *Aliyah never drank so this must be extremely difficult for her.* "You did not use a menu," observed Leda, "you must be familiar with this place."

Aliyah sensed the disappointment Leda could not hide. "Leda, Talib will call you exactly at one o'clock. We have about 50 minutes. I don't know what he will ask of you, but I know it will be incredibly dangerous. I told him I wanted to talk with you before he did. Leda, beware. I know you are trying to help our people but Talib is involved in a plot that can cause great harm. As your friend, as someone who loves you, please walk away from here and do not speak with him."

Leda could not reply in the flurry of two waiters putting down a half dozen dishes. "Aliyah, I know that Talib will require a great sacrifice. But I have thought about it for months and I have been positioning myself in the States to be of use to your cause. Why do you want to instill doubts in me when I have come to the conclusion that I am ready to do anything to further the cause of justice for the Palestinian people?"

"You are such a beautiful, brave idealist." Aliyah said this with tears in her eyes and Leda knew this was partially due to the unfamiliar effects of champagne.

"I feel it's my destiny and I feel comfortable with my decision. I can undertake any hardship this will involve." Leda said this with somewhat of a surprise at her own calm voice.

Aliyah took Leda's hand with a grasp that left it white, "You may be hurt, you will be in trouble with the law, and you know that military tribunals will not look kindly upon you. If this were just a criminal case, it would be child's play for someone of your wealth and social standing to get off. But Leda, here we are talking treason against your own country, terrorism!"

They picked at their food in silence. Leda was touched by her friend's concern but she expected praise and support, not this stony criticism. Finally Aliyah spoke, "And I certainly hope you are not doing this for Talib. I could see you were quite taken with him." Aliyah had hit a raw nerve.

"Of course not!" Leda said angrily taking another glass of champagne. "I have a desire to see justice and to do some good. Yes, Aliyah, good for my country, too. Our government at the highest levels has been duped." Leda saw a waiter approach, turned away, and continued in a much more subdued manner. "I'm ready to make a statement and I see myself more patriotic than all the silent flag-flying Americans that go along with anything propounded by the media." Leda exhaled vehemently and continued, "And as for Talib, of course I find him attractive. So do you. Are you jealous that he did not choose you? Or did he never even consider you as his avenging angel for the Palestinian people?"

Aliyah stood up, signaled the waiter, gave instructions to him in French, and turned to Leda. "If you think that I am discouraging you because of some type of jealousy on my part, instead of a sincere concern for your welfare, you misunderstand me so greatly that friendship between us is impossible."

The public telephone near her rang and a waiter picked it up. "Madame Lodge, for you." Aliyah turned and left.

"Leda, is Aliyah listening?"

Her hand was trembling holding the phone as she said, "No, she just left. But she was extremely negative about any participation I would have.

"Damn that woman!"

"What do you want of me? Will I see you?"

"No, Leda. You will never see me again. But you will be in my thoughts and heart every hour of every day for the rest of my life. You will also be a saint to the Palestinian people who will venerate you for all of history." She heard him inhaling on a cigarette and again asked him what she was to do. "You must be ready to sacrifice your life."

"I can hardly be a suicide bomber at the Conservative convention. The security will be very tight. Even with my connections, they have detectors, they have dogs...."

"No, no!" laughed Talib. "On the evening before the Conservative Convention in New York, Shlomo Weiss, the Israeli Prime Minister is to come to New York for a small, private dinner with the President and a group of major Jewish donors to the campaign. It is to be held in the Conservative Club." Leda was startled to find this out from Talib. She was a member of the club and had no idea.

"How do you know this?"

"I have my means. I also know that the highest security precautions will be taken. The FBI will comb every square inch of the facility and it will be equipped with the latest security devices. Armed agents will be posted everywhere and guests will need the highest security clearance. What I need from you, Leda is for you to be there."

"But I'm not Jewish. How would I get in?"

"I chose you darling because of your intelligence. You will find a way. And during dinner you will have one more chore. Start an accidental fire, a fire that will change history. That is all."

"Talib!" Leda exhaled.

"You have been there at their dinners. Start a significant fire where fire extinguishers would have to be used. I love you and may Allah protect you," concluded Talib before the line went dead.

She stumbled out into the bright, warm Parisian afternoon. A walk along the Seine revealed magnificent colors of the setting sun playing on the water and reflecting gold on the classic architecture of buildings and bridges. She saw the beauty that inspired all the French Impressionists with the juxtaposition of the image of burning flesh. She thought of Joan of Arc burned at the stake. The temperature rising, the cells separating, blood rushing to the area to help, skin blistering, exploding, coagulating, and the pain of being cooked alive.

But I will do this. I will not back out now. I have no alternative plan and my end is near. I will succeed in changing history. There are pills for pain. My education will not be wasted. I will know how to die. And the death will be for something, not a wasting away in some nursing home with my brain turning to mush. I must have an ingenious plan –a plan to start a fire.

She knew the fateful dinner would be at the Conservative Club. There would be the white and gold tablecloths and napkins embroidered with the Great Seal of the United States, the fresh flowers arranged artistically as centerpieces, and the hundreds of votive lights circling the great silver candelabra. In her mind's eye she saw the high-ceilinged ballroom, tablecloths, silver, flowers, and candles. That was the key and the solution.

And if I changed my mind? Calm down. Remember the Arab story told her by Talib: A powerful Caliph had a beloved donkey and his greatest desire was to communicate with this animal. A poor beggar named Ahmed went to the Caliph and said that he could teach the donkey to speak if he and the donkey had a magnificent palace, the best food, and three years to accomplish this feat. The Caliph agreed and said if he succeeded, Ahmed would get one half of the caliph's wealth, but if he failed, he would be beheaded. Ahmed moved into a brilliant palace with the donkey and they both had the best of everything. A year later, friends of Ahmed visited and discovered that the donkey had learned not one word. Worried, they asked Ahmed if he was not concerned about being beheaded. Ahmed answered, "I still have two years and in that time, who knows? The Caliph may die, or the donkey may die, or the donkey may learn how to speak." *Perhaps it would never happen.*

Returning to the hotel she found a message:

Leda, what a surprise! I am here in Paris on a good-will mission. My official duty of lunch with the French President's wife and a visit to an orphanage was yesterday. I am free for lunch. I am staying at the American Embassy. Call me. Amy Chester

After going through security at the American Embassy, which necessitated the removal of her Manolo Blhanik shoes, she was led into the private quarters of the Ambassador. Amy Chester, in a blue dress with spectacular gold Channel chains, came toward her with open arms. Leda met her with the customary air kisses.

"Amy, how did you know I was in Paris?"

"I called you at home and your housekeeper told me. I wanted you to chair a dinner for the Connecticut Conservative candidate for the Senate."

During lunch consisting of a glass of wine, a green salad, and a miniscule slice of quiche, Leda endeavored to turn the conversation to personal matters. "Amy, you know I'm a widow and a man I would really like to meet has happened on the scene, Senator Bloom of Michigan. Do you think you could possibly introduce us?"

"I'm shocked by your interest in him. He had been married for years to the love of his life, a beautiful blonde. After she died, he would not look at another woman. He had a brief marriage a few years ago, but it ended in a very bitter divorce. Besides, he's Jewish and I know you are a Catholic. He is in his middle eighties. What are you thinking of?"

"Please. I know this is difficult, but if you could just seat us together at the next fundraiser, I would do anything for you," Leda pleaded.

"I'll see what I can do. It may have to be a dinner at our home. He is not a very generous contributor, so he avoids fundraisers," Amy said as she rose from the table.

"I don't mean to impose on your good graces with my social needs."

"No problem at all. You've done so much for me and, who knows, you may be able to squeeze some money out of the old goat. After all he is as wealthy as Croesus."

Leda left the Embassy with a sense of accomplishment. Leda's heart was singing walking up the Avenue Montaigne. Looking in the windows of the couturiers, she thought, "Why not?"

The dress she wanted was very specific. It must be green with yards and yards of chiffon. The sleeves must be the voluminous, fashionable trumpets. They must look like angel wings when I raise my hands, she told the couturier. The waist must be very small and the décolletage must be very low. As the couturier was making the sketch Leda said, "Make the sleeves a little longer." He gave her a quizzical look. "Why, it is to hide my hands," Leda explained and the couturier understood." When will it be ready?"

"Oui, Madame, the fitting in muslin will be for the day after tomorrow. A work of art cannot be rushed, but we have never delivered a dress with three fittings in less than two weeks." Seeing the disappointment on Leda's face he added, "But Madame is such a perfect size that we could manage it in a week."

She had visions of enjoying Paris with Talib. Walking the wide boulevards, eating at the bistros, moonlight cruises on the Seine all ended with the desert of lovemaking on that luxurious bed at the Ritz. It would have been the highlight of her life before the final curtain descended. She needed company and found herself dialing Leslie's home number after the Gainer number did not answer.

Leslie answered. "Leslie, sleepyhead, what are you doing?"

"Leda, where are you?"

"In a beautiful late afternoon in Paris. Come join me. You need a break from your polling labors."

"I have a break. A permanent break I'm afraid. I started to question the polling and I got a golden parachute. You and all your conspiracy theories cost me my job."

Her next call was to Sophia and Conrad answered the phone. "How are you? Sophia and I were just discussing you and she did not want anyone to know but she got a horrendous diagnosis last week. Late stage ovarian cancer. See if there is anything you could do for her." Conrad said in a whisper.

"I want her to get on the next plane to Paris. Conrad, do not object. It is final. Put her on."

In a few minutes she heard Sophia, "Leda, I know he told you. I can't explain how I feel. I wish I were dead. Conrad keeps taking me to specialists who talk about experimental treatments and the new drugs which delay the progression. But Leda, you know the inevitable has started."

"Sophia, come to Paris. Today if you can get a flight. I am at the Ritz and absolutely need you here." Leda, as always, assumed that Sophia would be most vulnerable to someone else's need.

"Perhaps it would be good for me to escape reality for awhile. I'll see what I can do and call you back. Conrad will have to take full charge of the baby." A few hours later an excited Sophia called "I will be arriving tomorrow morning on Air France. I'll get a cab from De Gaulle and be at the Ritz around noon."

The two women had lunch at the Ritz and Leda confided everything to Sophia, but Sophia was not as shocked as she should have been. "Are you sure you don't think I am evil? I will be a mass murderer if I succeed." Leda wanted Sophia's unvarnished opinion.

"Who would ever suspect you, Leda? They will be on the lookout for young men of Middle Eastern descent as the perpetrators of any terrorist plot. As for evil, that is your private concern—a concern of your conscience and your communication with your Maker. Did Truman have these thoughts when he dropped the bomb on Hiroshima?"

"You have chosen your death and it will mean something. I have been handed my death and it will be far more painfully prolonged and will signify nothing and accomplish nothing," Sophia said as Leda asked if her sons knew. "My sons are concerned, but not with my feelings, just the logistics of treatment".

"And what about the new infant?"

"The baby is an enormous burden but there was no way I would let an innocent baby pay for Conrad's indiscretions." Tears rolled down Sophia's cheek as she thought of leaving the infant motherless.

"There is one favor I need from you, Leda. I need a prescription that I can fill here in France and take the drug home with me. When things get to the point where I can no longer live, I want to be able to end it all."

"I understand and will help you. Please, go to your room and take a nap. It's a long flight and you look exhausted."

Leda knew the lethal dose and wrote a prescription for continuous release morphine. She went to the local pharmacy, presented her medical credentials and explained that she needed this medication for the terminal pain of cancer. It was an emergency. The pharmacist came back with the small package. "I hope this helps, Doctor."

When Leda returned to the hotel, she warned, "These are very strong for pain, but if you crush them and take them, they are lethal. You understand me and I understand you. I fully agree with your wanting to be in control." Before giving the medicine to Sophia, Leda took half of the pills for herself.

The last week of happiness was filled with laughter, museums, lunches, and shopping. The dress fittings were a revelation to Leda. She never realized that the design could change her shape in such flattering ways. The bust was raised to reveal delicious half moons of sweet flesh, the waist slenderized, the figure elongated, and the flowing sleeves romantic. "The dress, she is perfection on you!" exclaimed the Master, and Leda nodded her head with a smile. *It should be for twenty thousand Euros.*

Dinner at the Jules Verne on top of the Eiffel Tower marked the end of their stay. The dining room was ultra modern in white and black. "Life was worth this week. It was perfect. Why was it so, Leda?"

"The imminent loss of everything makes it so much more alive and poignant. It is a shame we could not have lived out our entire lives in this state." Leda looked out at the lights of Paris and had a strong revelation of the beauty of life.

Sophie agreed, "No one could live their whole life at this intensity of feeling. It's reserved for a few moments, for a few glimpses into the eternal. It happens when you fall in love, when a child is born and when you know the end is at hand. Then every flower is a miracle, every person is unique, and every moment is precious."

CHAPTER 26

Leda needed to dispose her worldly goods. As a private person she wanted to erase all traces of herself. She gave away most of her furniture, books, clothes, dishes, and linens left with only her best bare necessities. She threw out all her papers and photographs. Why leave this to be done by someone else? All things we own are so transient, only to use for a little while. She might as well supervise the disposal according to her desires and direction. When she was questioned about her radical clean sweep she replied that she was going to do some redecorating. This answer satisfied everyone.

She had spent the last week in the library looking up all the news on Senator Bloom. She knew where he was born, his parent's names, his schools, his interests, and pet peeves. She had read that he fell in love with his first wife when she appeared in a white dress with violets in her hair. "I took one look at her and knew she was for me." Leda bought a form-fitting white dress would do but she was too old for violets so she substituted huge violet amethysts pointing down to her breasts. The self-tanner gave her a golden glow. She wore her big diamond bracelet and her largest diamond ring. Senator Bloom being from a poor family was impressed by wealth.

Security at the Chester's home, Blair House, was intense to the point of having her jewels examined and her evening bag almost torn apart. She was being patted down by a female Marine who seemed to enjoy running her fingers under her breasts saying, "Oh, I see a wire in the bra," when Amy came and extricated her.

The large, traditional room only had two other people beside the Vice-President and his wife. Leda was admiring the portraits on the wall when Amy rushed over. "Leda, you look stunning. Dick is very happy to have you here after all you had done for us." Dick Chester came closer and gave Leda a hug that she found a little too crushing for comfort. "Leda, this is Senator Perry and his wife, Mindy," stated Amy as she was leading her to the young couple. Senator Perry flashed Leda his practiced campaign smile and they shook hands. Mindy looked very stiff and uncomfortable in her baggy, grey dress and nodded shyly to Leda.

As Leda was making some comments to Mindy, she noticed two men enter the room. One was tall, handsome and distinguished with grey hair and a commanding presence, while the other was shapeless with a florid face and hooded eyes. She recognized Bloom immediately but had no clue to his striking companion.

"Well, Senator Bloom, you made it!" said Amy rushing over to give him an embrace.

"Amy, I hope you don't mind but I brought another guest,

Bradley Sears. We were in a planning meeting this afternoon and he mentioned what a fan he was of Dick. I told him I was invited to dinner tonight and I was sure you wouldn't mind. Do you?" Senator Bloom talked in a hoarse whisper as his eyes focused on Leda. She saw that he inadvertently licked his lips as he observed her.

"It would be a pleasure to entertain the CEO of Firewall Industries" gushed Amy who set about giving instructions to the maid about another place for dinner.

Senator Bloom walked directly to Leda and said, "So, you are the lady that Amy said wanted to meet me. I am flattered." Bradley Sears approached and Senator Bloom made the introductions. "Bradley is the Chairman of the American Israeli Political Action Committee. I don't know where he finds the time in addition to racking up his billions. He has made a fortune from Homeland Security, so he is also a patriot."

Leda made the appropriate flattering comments to Bradley and launched into a discussion about sailing with Senator Bloom. He started to smile and Leda saw his obvious dentures. Drinks were served and Bloom ordered a Manhattan. Leda followed suit. "It's so good to see a woman drinking hard liquor. My ex-wife stuck to white wine and I swear it pickled her into one old sour broad. Completely off the record of course," Bloom said with a nudge to Leda. "My first wife loved Martinis, bless her soul." Leda and Bloom got into a spirited conversation about how to make the best Martini.

Leda was seated between Bloom and Bradley but all her attention was focused on Bloom, which he appreciated, since Bradley was obviously superior in all the masculine traits. Dinner was standard fare. It was probably a dinner of the last minute to repay Leda and grant her wish. As Leda asked the right questions, Bloom could not stop talking. He didn't need conversation; he only needed a smiling, nodding audience. It helped when she asked questions that called for self-important answers.

Soon after the apple pie, the Vice-President excused himself saying he had some phone calls to make. She noticed Amy looking at her watch. Bradley excused himself saying his plane was waiting to take him home to Texas and he had not been home in a week due to his work in D.C. "Thank you for a memorable evening, Amy, and for the company. Could you call me a taxi?" Leda asked.

Amy got the hint and sprang into action. "Why Leda, Senator Bloom has his limousine waiting. I am sure the Senator would love to give you a lift to the Hay-Adams. It is on his way."

In the back seat of the limousine Leda mentioned her life-long desire to see Israel and how her support of the Conservative Party was always predicated on their stand on Israel. "Why that poor little country in the middle of all those violent Arabs," she said looking up at him.

As they reached the entry, she turned and said, "Can I buy you a nightcap, Senator? This hotel has an excellent bartender who makes fabulous Martinis and I would love your opinion on how I could be of help to Israeli causes."

Looking at her 10 carat diamond, Bloom said, "Why certainly Mrs. Lodge. May I call you Leda? You may call me Bloom, just Bloom. No Senator necessary between friends."

The bar was quiet. It was Tuesday evening and quite early—only 9:30. Leda speculated that Amy told her husband that it was just a "little dinner" so that he could work afterwards. The time of 6 pm was almost insulting. They may even have had another engagement. No matter, she got what she wanted. After two Martinis and a thorough discussion of Israeli politics, Leda leaned over and said, "I have the greatest desire to meet the Prime Minister. I would love to be able to see him just once in person. Do you have any idea when he is coming to the United States again?"

Bloom's turtle eyes opened and he said, "As a matter of fact, he will be here for the Conservative Convention. I believe Amy told me you are a member of the Conservative Club. There will be a dinner with President Brown. Of course tickets are a quarter of a million dollars. It is a very limited group."

"Just my luck," Leda said with a sigh.

"Well, if you wouldn't mind giving me a check I will get them to put another chair at the table. The tickets were sold out but I can get you in and the extra money will help Israel. It is tax-deductible, you know" he said with a wink as he patted her thigh.

"Thank you, Bloom. But I will not need the tax deduction. I will mail you my check in the morning and I will write it out to you so you would be free to dedicate the money to where it will do the most good. You are so brilliant."

"You are a very crafty lady. I will enjoy getting to know you." The pressure on her thigh was increasing and moving upward and only the arrival of the waiter with the check stopped the hand's progress.

Leda signed the bill to her room and stood up and looked at the disappointed face of Bloom. "I'm glad Amy invited you. Will Vice-President Chester be at the dinner with the President and the Prime Minister?"

"No, only the President will be there because you know they could never attend the same functions together due to security reasons." With this they made plans to meet in New York and Bloom gave Leda his card with his personal number. "Call me, anytime" he said with a wink.

🔥

Returning to Connecticut, home never seemed safer, or more inviting, after having disposed of the non-essentials. *Everyone loses everything in the end. We only borrow our earthly possessions. But what pleasure they brought me.* It was more painful to contemplate a fiery death. She ran her fingers over the contours of her face, and enveloped herself in an embrace. But loss of her body would come anyway. The pain, she could control the pain. Leda lit a cigarette and placed the match next to her little finger. She did not feel anything for the first few seconds then the throbbing started. In the pharmacy text she studied the onset times of various morphine dosages. She ground her French morphine pills into a powder and placed it into three capsules.

An appointment at Smythe, Smythe and Tillman with her attorney to update her will and her funeral arrangements was next. Leda sat across a vast polished mahogany. The décor of the room was meant to convey seriousness and limitless wisdom. The money from her estate would go to UNWRA, the United Nations Refugee Fund, designated for Palestinian refugees. "You really care about those people," remarked Jim Smythe. He had been the family attorney for two generations and now he appeared as a wizened oracle. "Are you sure this is what Arthur would have wanted? You've been spending so much money on political activity and now this inclusion of the United Nations in your will. Arthur must be turning over in his grave. I cannot imagine him approving."

"Jim, Arthur would want me to do what I think is right. I really don't need your advice on this. One more thing, Jim. I would like to set up a trust for any animals that are alive when I die in care of Rhoda so she would not feel a financial burden. Let's say a thousand dollars a month for the next ten years. That will certainly outlive the lifetimes of the pets and provide a little cushion for Rhoda."

"Nothing else?"

"No, Jim. That's it."

An air of unreality settled on Leda as if she were observing her own actions from a distance. She swerved from delusions of grandeur to fears of insanity. On especially good days when she woke in the morning, she was so glad to be alive, carefree. She had energy pulsing through her with joy, *what am I doing*?

Then she would see cruelty everywhere in the world. Driving home from the appointment with her attorney, she saw a mother duck and six ducklings attempting to cross a highway. She slowed down, but the car next to her sped up and crushed three of them. At the next red light she saw two teens laughing. The world is full of pain. We live by the grace of a happy blindness but eyes grow out of our souls in times of pain and panic. With these eyes we can see the world in darkness as it really is.

The engraved invitation came and the hazy thoughts of an intellectual plot, idealistic reasons, and pretend assassinations sharpened into a clear focus of burning flesh and multiple deaths.

Reality had arrived.

CHAPTER 27

A final morning walk-through of her home of 30 years, a pat on the head to her dog and her cat, a farewell hug to Rhoda before she left in a hired car for The Helmsley Palace Hotel. She did not want to leave her car stranded in a city parking lot. *Why did I care what happened to the car?* Arriving at the hotel, the bellboy helped her with her luggage as she entered the suite and unpacked. A Madison Avenue hairdresser arrived and performed his miracles. A bath and make-up, components of daily life, took on new meaning. *I will never repeat this ritual again.*

At six, she put on her green gown and decided to look in the mirror. It was painful to lose herself. She looked exquisite. *It is better to depart from this life in my current state than in a hospital gown with a diaper not knowing who I am. I will avoid years of care by strangers.* Years and decades pass and people vegetate, but at some moments people live a life of a higher order. Is it true that life is ninety-nine percent boredom and one percent panic?

She remembered Arthur's disapproval of terrorism and was shaken with doubt. *Arthur, you truly loved me and understood my soul but I know you would not stop me now since I am coming to join you.* She achieved peace with this justification. Some turmoil was still present and she fell to her knees and begged God to tell her if she was doing the right thing. No reply was heard.

She took her jeweled evening purse with the three large capsules inside the lining. The medicine would work within a few minutes but she wanted to be drug-free for security.

The limousine she took had trouble getting within two blocks of the event. Traffic was at a standstill. Furthest away, contained by helmeted, armed national guard and horse-mounted policemen, were about a hundred people with anti-war signs and a few scraggly demonstrators wearing the kaffiyah and shouting, "Long live the intifada!" The limousine driver saw the group and said to Leda, "They should be sent back to where they came from. I hate all these protestors. I was one myself during Vietnam. But now it is a different situation. We are at war with terror." Closer to the event was a mass of hundreds of people waving the Israeli flag and shouting, "Friendship eternal, Brown and Weiss!"

At the checkpoint Leda was examined and she showed her invitation. Thank God she had also brought her photo ID, which was examined for a long time by a policeman who then handed it over to a plainclothes detective. "Ma'am, sorry to put you through this but you must understand that security is at the highest levels." Leda could also see men with machine guns everywhere. "Sorry, the whole area has been cordoned off. Your car cannot enter any further. You will have to walk or have one of our men escort you in this golf cart." He then took out a sheet of paper and ran down the names and read, Mrs. Leda Lodge, 65, green eyes, 130 pounds. He looked her up and down. "Again sorry, ma'am, but you understand."

Security took her in the golf cart through the streets of this unusually warm September evening. Her thoughts were on a roller coaster. *I will be a historical figure. How many people have the opportunity to change history? The Palestinians will know that someone died for their nation, their freedom. But here in America I will be vilified as a traitor. Am I betraying my country? No, No, No! I am just directing it upon a better and more just path.*

The golf cart stopped in front of the door and Leda saw the whole lobby as a huge screening area. They checked her name, the photo ID, the x-ray machine, the sniffing dogs and finally a woman frisked Leda thoroughly. She took away her compact because of the powder. The security officer also examined her lipstick and drove a straight pin through the middle. "It could harbor a bullet," she said by way of explanation. Leda finally retrieved her shoes and entered. Walking through the lobby, she was aware she was creating a stir—the flowing chiffon gown, the gold and emerald earrings and necklace, and the stature of a queen. Her posture was perfection and now there was no turning back.

She walked up to the seating chart and saw that she was at Table #1. She opened the door to the ballroom and saw the multitude of round tables decorated with blue and white flowers, and masses of blue and white votive candles, the colors of the Israeli flag. Table #1 was placed in front next to the long, raised table with American and Israeli flags. *Luck is with me so far.* A man came up to her and said, "Cocktails this way. No one is allowed in there now."

The cocktail room was a sea of black and she realized she would be one of the few women present with only the empress of a cosmetics empire and the wife of a casino mogul. There were about 100 people there that would fill the coffers by a cool 25 million. Bloom saw her and in a booming voice said, "Leda, you look stunning!"

"Why Senator, it is marvelous to be included." She walked up to the bar with him and had her last Martini. *The frozen glass, the ice crystals floating in the vodka, the blue cheese stuffed olives. No wonder Arthur called it liquid happiness. On my empty stomach, this drink will take the edge off and potentiate the morphine.* "I will have another." He introduced her to quite a few men but she did not remember their names. Memory depends upon interest. There would be no need to remember.

Dinner was announced with great excitement mounting in the well-lubricated crowd, Leda was surprised that she felt a passing desire for some food. The most prosaic considerations of the flesh sometimes intrude on the most magnificent phenomenon of the spirit.

Entering the ballroom, it took awhile before everyone was seated. With great fanfare the double doors opened and a cadre of secret service with their microphones behind their ears entered. The agents already in place around the perimeter of the room stood at attention. Four men entered with Uzi machine guns. Bloom turned to her and said, "This is a trifle overdone but Israeli security insisted." Finally both heads of state entered to a standing ovation. President Brown looked just as he did on television and was much taller than she expected as he walked by her. Shlomo Weiss was a good looking, short man with the orange undertones of a self-tanner. As he passed, he winked at Leda, leaving a trace of cologne. They sat down at the head table.

The American anthem was followed by the Israeli anthem. A rabbi gave the invocation, which called on God's blessings to protect Israel from harm. Dinner consisted of a smoked salmon appetizer and filet mignon with vegetables. Leda played with her food and took a bite of the filet. Bloom noticed and said, "So that is how you keep your magnificent figure," eyeing her breasts.

Leda saw that neither Brown nor Weiss really ate due to the prolonged whispered conversation between them. As coffee was beginning to be served, they gave speeches in turn. President Brown sang the endless song of cooperation and eternal friendship. *Would eliminating these two kindly middle-aged men really change the course of history? Yes! Their bland exterior was just a mask for their hideous plans for war and injustice. They operated under a cover of good while they were plotting to eliminate all who stood in their way. As Talib said, we must cut off the heads of the snake.*

Leda turned toward Bloom and with her hand on his knee said, "Excuse me while I powder my nose." As she walked out of the ballroom, she had a vision of death. The death of her mother, of Arthur, of Yasmin—they were all so ugly. She could still stop this onrushing locomotive. *What is my alternative ending? This is my fate and I submit.*

In the Ladies room two women agents were observing Leda closely. She went into the stall, lifted her dress, sat down, extracted the capsules and swallowed. She flushed the toilet and exited smiling. She stopped to look at herself in the mirror while taking a plastic cup filled with water and then yet another to wash the bitter powder down. She smiled at one of the security guards; "Smoked salmon makes me so thirsty."

It is done, no more thoughts, no more love, no more me. At last I find peace.

As she walked back to her place at the table, Prime Minister Weiss was thanking all the contributors and said he appreciated their support in his re-election bid against Jacob Herzog. "All the polls show me beating him by forty percent! So you see I don't really need your money!" This was met with raucous laughter and clapping.

Leda felt very warm and flushed, the morphine starting to take effect. She was feeling free as if she were starting to float above the whole scene. *To depart from this life with such a grand gesture!* This thought was becoming hazy. *Now, Leda, Now! This is the moment of death. Death is not darkness, its approach seen only in the eyes of cats and owls. No! Death is a swirl of colors and laughter and light. It is a metamorphosis of the butterfly from its cocoon. Death at the hands of history is the only death containing the seeds of life. I will have the perfect death—swift, powerful and historic. Arthur always called me a perfectionist and now here was my final proof.* Her eyes started glazing and she only saw Arthur beckoning her to him. *I believe in God the Father Almighty, Creator of heaven and earth and in His Son, Jesus Christ, conceived by the Virgin Mary, crucified, died and was buried and descended into hell and on the third day he arose from the dead, according to the scriptures... descended into*

Hell! What was He doing in Hell? Is that where she was now? Is there hell to every death?

"The salmon was quite salty," whispered Leda, pointing to her empty water glass. Bloom signaled the waiter. As the waiter was pouring the water, Leda stood up, reached over to the flowers saying, "These flowers are beautiful!" She seemed to be attempting to remove one white lily from the centerpiece when her long chiffon sleeve dipped into the votive candle. An instant blaze erupted in the thin chiffon fabric. When she dropped her arm to her skirt the whole dress went up in flames. Within seconds she was a human fireball.

She screamed at the searing pain and tried to put her hands up to protect her face and her burning hair. The secret service jumped into action, grabbing the numerous fire extinguishers prominently displayed on the walls. As they squirted the fire retardant at Leda she gasped breathing the gas. One agent threw Leda to the floor and covered her with his jacket while the spraying went on. The toxic fumes burned her inside and proved more fatal than the fire. Leda was carried out to the street wrapped in a blanket.

A massive coughing could be heard throughout the room. The fire was extinguished but panicked people began to breathe the poisonous fumes and were shouting and screaming. Their eyes and throats were burning and most were in a stampede to escape as they trampled one another in their panic security was shouting into their radios for help. Brown and Weiss were surrounded by security as they gasped and collapsed.

The two heads of state were carried out, pushing away other panicked people. Some agents had broken the large windows for fresh air. It was pandemonium. An agent yelled, "The President is not breathing!" as he performed CPR. The area was surrounded and ambulances had a hard time entering. A helicopter landed on Fifth Avenue, and Brown and Weiss were whisked away to Columbia-Presbyterian Hospital where all hands were put on red alert. Leda on a gurney was taken to Lennox Hill Hospital where her death was pronounced.

No one in the first few minutes could figure out what had happened. There was wild speculation of sabotage, a terrorist attack, a tragic accident. At midnight the news media announced the death of the American President and the critical injury of the Prime Minister of Israel. The news stories started with, "The unfortunate fire leading to the discharge of as yet an unidentified poison in the fire extinguishers." Three days later the Prime Minister died. The death toll stood at eight with ten still critical and sixty-one people hospitalized.

The minute Aliyah heard the news on Al-Jazeera she knew that Leda had gone ahead with it. *Why did she not listen to my warning? It is I who am at fault. I am responsible for my friend's death.*

The press studied Leda's background, interviewing her friends. Leslie reached at a tennis camp in South America, registered shock and said that Leda was a patriot, a strict Conservative, and a good Catholic. Certainly she had nothing to do with the tragic, recent events.

Mary in Florida was preening before the cameras for her fifteen minutes of fame, "No, Leda was an average American. I knew her for years and there was nothing to indicate her being involved in any subversive plot."

Sophia did know and was amazed at what Leda had done but asked Conrad to spare her the interviews. She hated the media intrusion. "I am sorry, but my wife is ill. She has end stage ovarian cancer and cannot be interviewed," mumbled Conrad with a lowered head.

Amy still couldn't believe that she was moving into the White House. This elevation in status was beyond her wildest dreams. Her husband was now the President. Leda must have been involved. The fire extinguishers would not have been used without a fire. But why? There were rumors that she had left her estate to UNRAW. In her wildest imagination Amy Chester could not see Leda in the role of a terrorist. She was so conventional, so restricted to conservative causes. In an interview Amy distanced herself from Leda, "Yes, Dr. Eimont was a generous contributor to Conservative causes but I know thousands of people in that category."

At FBI headquarters, the investigation was at full throttle. They still could not trace the poison used since the only prototype was a military grade top- secret chemical weapon. The fire extinguishers came from the largest manufacturer of fire extinguishers in the country, Firewall Industries. Just five days before the dinner the FBI had replaced them with new ones certified by Firewall Industries. They had passed every inspection and had not been any place where they could have been tampered with. How could they have been switched? Bradley Sears, CEO of Firewall Industries, was interviewed and said that a thorough investigation was being done.

The investigation led to a disgruntled Firewall employee, John Molloy, who had brief access placing labels on the batch of fire extinguishers and was a chemistry genius in school.

Further research into his computer records revealed a search for poisons. He was known to be a violent critic of government policies and had made statements about his disgust with President Brown. In his twenties he had had psychiatric care. However, before he could be interviewed, he had a fatal car accident on the Taconic Parkway. His blood alcohol level was three times the legal limit. His wife denied that her husband had any possible involvement claiming he did not even drink. "You are making a scapegoat of my husband and he did not have anything to do with this."

A friend of Malloy, Jimmy Smith, had been a waiter at the Republican dinner that night and it was speculated that, in bringing the water to Leda, he pushed her into the flame. Unfortunately, he was nowhere to be found and there was a trail of false documents that indicated he never existed.

Although there was much speculation about conspiracy theories, implicating Chester, the one who benefited by this tragedy, the investigation lost steam.

Senator Bloom was considered a hero having not only survived the attack, but also heroically saving three other people. A new law was introduced by Senator Bloom to prevent fire extinguisher tampering, which required inspections of all fire extinguishers by Homeland Security. The law passed unanimously by the House and Senate. Senator Bloom maintained Leda, his guest, was entirely innocent and a victim of Mr. Molloy's terroristic plot to kill President Brown.

The war on terrorism was now was on red alert.

Eventually, the FBI and CIA reached the conclusion that Leda was involved somehow although they had no definitive proof, only circumstantial evidence. However, there could have been no poisoned fire extinguishers without a fire. She had left a trail of preparing for her demise and her trips to the Middle East were uncovered. The media needing someone to blame, a face to put to the horrific act, jumped on the idea that Leda masterminded the whole incident. Leda would be remembered forever as a traitor, a murderer, and a terrorist. The Palestinians only associated Leda with further draconian measures against them. Only the Mossad had authority to investigate in Israel and after questioning Aliyah they could not reach any conclusions. There was no record of Talib according to the Mossad and due to a request from the highest sources of Israeli government the investigation came to a sudden halt.

EPILOGUE

In Paris at the Alexandria Cafe a handsome young man with flashing brown eyes sat at a small corner table near a window overlooking the dark, wet winter morning. He put down his newspaper with the screaming headlines. *All that was organized in Damascus has succeeded and protection from the Mossad at the highest levels gives me immunity. Now the reward.*

He looked up as a man with salt and pepper hair carrying a black alligator suitcase approached. They stood in Seville Row suits shaking hands as their thin gold watches flashed, out of place in this poor neighborhood.

"Talib, congratulations." Placing the black alligator briefcase from under the table, Bradley Sears of Firewall Industries said, "Here it is, the numbers of the three wire accounts totaling 100 million in Cyprus. Just as you asked. A lot of money but it is worth it for the cause – a return of Israel's ancient glory."

"You got what you paid for. I still do not understand

why a man as popular as Prime Minister Weiss had to be eliminated."

"Our party felt that Weiss was so popular he would have been reelected. But he was too soft, and was not moving fast enough for a Greater Israel and now we will have Herzog who vows to clean out the West Bank and Gaza."

They both ordered espresso as Talib pointed to the headlines in the paper. "The media believes the American President was the target."

"He was collateral damage. If we had eliminated Weiss any other venue, it would have been called an Israeli plot blaming Herzog. They would have seen it as his gain by Weiss' death."

Talib took this news in stride as he lit another cigarette. "Now I can pay off some of my gambling debts and get out of that hell-hole of the Middle East."

Bradley ordered another espresso. "I see that they know their coffee in this dump."

"How did you get Malloy?"

After a sip he said, "I had to personally oversee the operation and Malloy was the perfect suspect- reclusive, a loner. We filled his computer with classified chemical compound formulas and it was a done deal. Eliminating him and Jimmy Smith was child's play."

"How did you switch the fire extinguishers?"

"We never switched them. We were counting on not having to use them. A woman on fire justified their use. That woman was a stroke of luck." Bradley smiled, twirling his cup.

"Yes, she was crucial. We needed someone above suspicion. Now there is a question of involvement but so what she is dead. She was naïve and an easy target as are most idealists. He shifted to avoid the sudden ray of sunlight, "Seduction of an old woman is really hard work."

"Enjoy your gains and remember that Herzog and our people are grateful. We are looking forward to a rebuilding of our Temple in Jerusalem."

In response to his people's cries for more security in the face of the loss of their beloved leader, the new Prime Minister of Israel, Jacob Herzog, put all Palestinians under detention and started to clear all Palestinians out of Israel.

"There is enough room in Jordan for all of them."

President Chester agreed. No country objected.

THE END